Carli planned to be a Good Samaritan. . .but she opened a can of worms instead.

Carli slipped into her coat, smoothed on gloves, then exited the apartment by the back entrance, skirted the side of the building, cut across the damp, spongy lawn and approached the rental agency vehicle from the rear, coming up on the driver's side.

She pecked on the window.

The gentleman who'd been reading, with the use of a small penlight, almost jumped out of his skin at the unexpected noise.

He pressed a button and the window slid down.

"I couldn't help noticing that you've been parked here all afternoon," Carli blurted. "Are you lost? May I help you?"

Before the startled man could answer, Carli saw that *The Wall Street Journal* and *USA Today* had been neatly folded and placed on the passenger side, and it was a well-worn Bible that the old man had been reading with the aid of a small flashlight. She felt a rush of commonality with him, a trust that was instinctive when dealing with others whom she recognized as believers.

"Actually, Miss, I'm waiting for someone to arrive home. An old friend. I'd been told that this was where he lived. Maybe my source was incorrect."

"I know most of the people in the apartment house," Carli said. "Who are you looking for?"

"Austin Dennis. . .do you know him? Does he live here?"

For a moment Carli felt weak-kneed. "Yes. . .he does. . .we do. . .I'm his wife."

D0752822

BRENDA BANCROFT is the pen name of inspirational romance author Susan Feldhake. At home in central Illinois with her husband, Steven, and four children, she is employed as a writing instructor for a college-accredited correspondence school. In her spare time, she likes to hike, listen to country and western music, and fellowship with close friends.

Other books by Brenda Bancroft

Don't miss out on any of our super romances. Write to us at the following address for information on our newest releases and club information.

Heartsong Presents Readers' Service
PO Box 719
Uhrichsville, OH 44683

Once More
With Feeling

Brenda Bancroft

Heartsong Presents

A note from the author:
I love to hear from my readers! You may correspond with me
by writing: **Brenda Bancroft**
Author Relations
PO Box 719
Uhrichsville, OH 44683

ISBN 1-57748-332-4

ONCE MORE WITH FEELING

© 1998 by Barbour Publishing, Inc. All rights reserved. Except
for use in any review, the reproduction or utilization of this work
in whole or in part in any form by any electronic, mechanical, or
other means, now known or hereafter invented, is forbidden
without the permission of the publisher, Heartsong Presents,
PO Box 719, Uhrichsville, Ohio 44683.

All of the characters and events in this book are fictitious. Any
resemblance to actual persons, living or dead, or to actual events
is purely coincidental.

Cover illustration by Kay Salem.

PRINTED IN THE U.S.A.

one

The spring day couldn't have been more lovely as Carli Waggoner and Gus Dennis strolled out of their small neighborhood church in a rural Virginia town.

Old Union Christian Church was a small house of worship, solidly constructed with clapboard siding kept pristinely painted by the church family. Neatly pruned juniper shrubs hugged the solid, older building. Stained glass windows were kept in shining perfection by the women, as were the flower beds that hovered around the sign displaying the church's identity, pastor's name, and times of services. But it was the lilacs, wafting their special aromatic bouquet from the hedge running along the edge of the church property, that gave everything a special sweet promise that early May day.

Old Union Christian Church was modestly appointed. It reflected the incomes of most of the congregation—bluecollar working people, where men supported their families, and women carefully managed paychecks so they could stay home and be full-time mothers and homemakers. And it was a community of believers rich in blessings of faith whatever else they might lack.

Other members of the church choir had chatted with Carli Waggoner and Gus Dennis both before and after services and they'd spent a few moments talking to Pastor Meyer, who had taken the call to their church about the same time that Carli and Gus had met and begun attending.

Carli had moved to the area from the coal mining region of Kentucky. Gus had lingered on in the Virginia region, inland, instead of near the ocean where he'd served four years with the Atlantic Fleet, assigned to the turbine crew on the *U.S.S. Thorn*.

Holding hands, Carli and Gus were walking toward Gus's older, but well-maintained car that he'd bought during his last year in the Navy. With what he made as the manager of a local pizza chain, he probably could've afforded a newer, fancier model, but Gus had an appreciation for the quiet comforts in life. One of the things that had drawn Carli to him was that he chose function ahead of flashiness, and was content with what he had, desiring nothing more, wanting nothing less, considering that whatever his specific lot in life at the moment, it was his as ordained by a loving, caring Father Who sought to bring Gus to mature faith through life's circumstances.

Decent. Durable. Determined. Dedicated. Devout.

In Carli's eyes, that description was a thumbnail sketch of Austin Dennis III, the sometimes frustrating, frequently enigmatic man she found herself helpless not to love and accept. . .his few faults and all.

"Carli! Gus! Wait up—please!" Terri Bingham cried, as she and several of the youngsters from the Youth Fellowship came chasing after them.

"Could you come to the meeting tonight as Youth Fellowship chaperones?" The teenagers begged, explaining that one of the regulars had been unexpectedly called out of town for a family emergency.

"It's okay by me," Gus agreed. "Tonight's my night off. Carli?"

"Sure! Sounds like fun. We'll be there."

"We'll feed you supper!" Terri promised, delivering the statement almost like a wheedling bribe.

"Good deal. Uh. . .just make sure it's not pizza," Gus teased, lifting his arms and acting like he was tossing a crust.

A few of the teenagers whom he'd employed at the pizzeria followed suit until they all looked like they were kindergartners doing an elaborate finger play.

"Someone better remember to order a cheeseburger and fries for Gus," another pointed out. "Because we were planning on a pizza party."

"Hey—pizza's okay," Gus assured. "Just make sure it's the right brand, the place where we all work!"

Laughing, Gus held the car door for Carli, then went around

and seated himself behind the wheel.

"Where to for Sunday dinner?" he asked.

"My place," Carli said. "I put a pot roast in the oven at dawn and added potatoes and carrots before you picked me up for services."

"A home-cooked meal!" Gus said, sighing, inhaling deeply, as if he could actually smell the succulent odors. "You're a woman after my own heart. Actually, you've had my heart for a long, long time," he said softly.

Carli gave him a gently amused smile and squeezed his right hand that rested between them on the car seat.

"I want a gal, just like the gal, who didn't marry dear old Dad!" He paraphrased the old lyrics.

Before Carli could use that rare remark as a springboard to ask Gus about his family, an area that he generally kept off-limits, he spoke.

"Let's get married, Carli," Gus suddenly proposed, although it didn't really come as a surprise to either of them. "What do you say?"

"Oh, Gus!" Carli gasped.

For a moment she could hardly breathe as happiness over-took her. He hadn't yet started the car and she threw her arms around his neck, solidly kissing his cheek. He shifted slightly and their lips sweetly connected.

"Am I to assume that means. . .yes?"

"Yes. . .oh, yes. . .!"

"Then we have our plans for the afternoon," Gus said, happily taking her hand, kissing its soft palm, then closing her fingers around the area as if to place it in safekeeping. "After my beloved fixes me an all-American Sunday dinner, then we can go ring shopping. How does that sound?"

"Like a dream come true!"

"And then later on we'll return to the church to chaperone the Youth Fellowship. We can practice so we'll be old hands at dealing with kids when we have children of our own."

"Babies come with diapers when you watch them for others," Carli said, "from what some of the women in the choir have said, I think teenagers are equipped with 'attitudes'.

The way I hear their favorite pastimes are squabbling with parents whom they consider controlling, manipulating, and meddling. While it's pretty clear to me that their parents are only responding out of loving concern and Christian convictions in wanting what's best for their children."

For a moment Gus was silent and reflective and Carli realized that she'd blithely traipsed into what she knew could be touchy territory with Gus: talk of parents!

She realized that, without meaning to, she'd sent Gus's thoughts spiraling back to his childhood in the Northeast that he simply didn't talk about.

It'd seemed automatic for him to introduce her to some of his old buddies from the Navy who'd remained with the fleet in the Norfolk area, and to people at his job, but it was as if his family had failed to exist because he wished to escape whatever their influence had once been.

From a few words spoken in her presence during her childhood, Carli knew that familial relationships were often not what one could desire. Her own father's family was proof of that. Growing up to become a coal miner himself, Clayton Waggoner had been raised in a coal-mining family. His father and mother had married young, worked hard, too hard, and adversity had been a constant in their lives. His father, perhaps too young to shoulder the responsibility of so many mouths to feed, and during a time of volatility and violence in the coal mines, had one day simply disappeared.

No one knew if he was among the "agitators" silenced by men in positions of power, far removed from the coal mines, or if he'd simply turned his back on his family in Kentucky and sought a fresh start and new beginning elsewhere.

Little did it matter, for it left Elvira Waggoner and her seven children, of whom Clayton was the eldest, destitute and desperate in a time before social programs came to the aid of the impoverished and abandoned. Elvira placed her children in foster homes, then fled the Appalachian region herself. Clayton, the eldest child, ran away from the home that was no home to him and as scarcely a youth set about making his way in a grown man's world.

He lost all contact with his brothers and sisters, had no knowledge of how to locate them, but a few times remarked that he hoped that his siblings had fared better in foster homes than had he, and that they'd been taken in by people who loved and cared for them, and not just the stipend they received for sheltering an unwanted youngster.

While Clayton and Coralee Waggoner had given Carli what seemed an idyllic childhood, she was aware that not all children possessed such happy memories of their childhood years.

By the time she was in grade school she was aware that certain children tended to come to school with bruises—put there by a parent—and that more than a few children cringed when the teacher raised her voice to the class in general, for at home they received such railing tirades of criticism and name-calling that they felt unworthy to even be around other people.

By the time graduation had rolled around, some of them were already married with children, having sought to escape their parents by having their own households, only to find the cycle continuing. Some had run away. A few had been taken away—by police escort.

Carli realized that it was her father's Christian beliefs that had saved his soul—but also saved him as a human being—for he had found true forgiveness for what choices his young parents had made in life.

"They didn't mean their young'uns no harm," he quietly said a time or two when it seemed that the old feelings and emotions welled up until there was no way to remain silent any longer. "God have mercy on 'em. They did the best they knew how. Mayhap they were only passin' along the ways of their own raising."

And Clayton Waggoner considered himself a man blessed that a good woman like Coralee Baker had come into his life, her and her beloved Christ, and showed him a different way to life, a different family to which to belong, so that with Carli he felt that he was breaking an ongoing cycle. A cycle that Carli's mama had nodded about and referred to as "intergenerational bondage," big words that Carli didn't understand, but knew, somehow, was a sad sickness of the soul that passed on for generations who lived without the healing presence of God in their lives.

Gus had committed his life to the Lord. But what had his family done that had so embittered him that it was as if he wanted to "shake the dust off his feet" and never return? Carli was aware that the times that her father had talked about his childhood, while rare, had actually seemed to be very healing experiences for him. And it had made those around him love and admire and appreciate him all the more for the forces he'd struggled against and survived.

Dare she press Gus for answers? Frankly let him know that she understood how skewed family dynamics could be at times? Was their relationship such now, with the commitment of marriage, that she dared press for deeper answers, and not settle for the remark that Gus had once made: "Some kids have long, happy childhoods. Mine was long. . . ?"

Before she could reach a decision Gus spoke.

"If we're lucky," Gus said a moment later, his voice light, although a dark shadow seemed to remain in his eyes, "perhaps we'll get a chance to see the Reverend Rollie tonight and give him the good news, and make arrangements for a wedding."

"Won't the kids be excited?" Carli suggested, and decided to postpone confronting Gus about his past and his relationship with his parents.

"No more excited than we are!" Gus assured.

At Carli's apartment, Gus put CDs in the compact disc player, then attractively set the table in the tiny kitchenette as nearby Carli fussed over the last-minute meal preparations on the small gas range. Within a few minutes, steaming plates and bowls graced the table. Gallantly Gus held the chair for Carli to seat herself, then took a chair across from her. They smoothed their paper napkins on their laps, then Gus said grace before Carli served food from the cheap, colorful four-piece china set that Carli had bought at the local discount store.

"I've never had a better meal in my entire life," Gus said, putting his arm around Carli's waist as she poured him a second cup of flavored coffee and replaced the container of cream into the tiny refrigerator after they'd both lightened their coffee.

"Just the first of many," Carli said. "Now I know what Mama meant when she said that there was joy in feeding a man with an appreciation for good food. My mama was a fine cook."

"I have a hunch you're going to be her equal, sweetheart," Gus predicted.

"I have her recipes," Carli said.

"I wish I could've met your parents," Gus said. "I think I'd have loved such good, simple folks. And your father could've taught me some tricks on the fiddle."

"You'll learn," Carli said, laughing when she remembered the day when they'd been poking around in a quaint, antique shop in a tiny Virginia town that time seemed to have passed by.

There had been an instrument, the owner had described it as a violin. Gus had seemed drawn to it. It was terribly out of tune when he applied the bow. For an instant—it sounded like a violin—but then as Gus frowned, and began to saw away in a different manner, it caused a lump to form in Carli's throat, it so reminded her of her late father and his fiddling techniques.

"I think I can learn to do this and enjoy it!" Gus had said, determinedly. "I'll take it!"

"You'd have liked my father," Carli murmured in an emotion-laden tone. "Mama, too. Salt of the earth, the both of them. You'll get to know them someday come Glory. . ."

"We won't have families to worry about getting to the wedding, will we?" Gus said, his tone rueful, a bit sad.

"No." Gus already knew of the dispersion of the Waggoner side of the family, and her mother's people, while loving and caring, were few in number and reduced down to a couple of old-maid aunts who lived in a sheltered-care home near Nashville.

"You could invite your family, Gus," Carli ventured. "After all, I'd be marrying into your family line, and—"

"No!" his voice grew uncharacteristically steely. "I won't inflict them on the woman I love! They'd make you miserable. You'd rue the day you ever laid eyes on them. And—"

There was such a flash of determined dread that Carli didn't even consider dissuading him, her hopes for a healing reconciliation quietly and quickly abandoned.

"We have lots of friends," she reminded. "And our church family."

"Hopefully some of my buddies in Norfolk can get leave to come for the occasion."

"We'll do our best. Perhaps Reverend Rollie can assist us so that we can arrange dates so *The Thorn* won't be out on a Middle East cruise or something."

"Lord willing, it'll all work out. I'll check with the guys and see what's on their cruise schedule. I don't think they have a six-month deployment until autumn."

Gus's friends had become Carli's, too. In fact, it was through one of his friends that they'd met. One of his buddies had a weekend pass, so he'd made the trip to visit Gus. A serviceman raised in a background not unlike Carli's, where church attendance was an integral part of daily life, he'd sought out a place to attend worship services and had been drawn to Old Union Christian Church. He'd brought Gus with him.

Carli noticed the man in his Navy dress uniform and the well-dressed fellow with him, who had brown hair with sun-streaked tips, a deep tan, and an athletic physique.

She was unaware that the quiet stranger had noticed her, too, until his face was familiar when he returned for Wednesday night services. It was customary for the choir director to approach newcomers and invite them to join the choir, especially if she'd heard good sounds coming from their directions in the pews, and before long Gus was asked if he'd like to join the choir.

Gus was a wonderful addition to the choir. In addition to his rich baritone voice, they were delighted to learn of Gus's organ abilities one Sunday morning when the church's organist was stricken with flu symptoms, and was unable to take her place at the keyboard. Gus, who had admitted he was "pretty good at sight-reading," had handily performed so that they had musical accompaniment for the services.

Gus admitted to liking to move around and explore different places and get to know "the real people who populate the country." But any notions about moving on seemed to be abandoned once Carli entered his life.

From then on it was as if Carli Waggoner and the Lord were consuming anchors in his life. Gus's home life may not have been much when he was growing up, but he basked in the unconditional love of the church family congregation. At times Carli thought that she and Gus were like the cherished kids that some of the people in the church had never had, and they enjoyed the young couple's company like surrogate parents would.

"We'll have our church family to celebrate with us," Carli said.

"It'll be a day to remember when we get married."

"Memorable for the rest of our lives."

"I don't want us to wait too long," Gus said, and cupped his hand at the nape of Carli's neck and drew her soft lips to his, kissing her until she was short of breath.

"Me neither."

"Then what do you say we go in search of the perfect ring, my sweet?" Gus said, and released Carli from his quick embrace, even though it was clear that he'd have enjoyed holding her forever.

"I say. . .okay. But don't overspend, honey. We have so many more important things that we'll need."

"I know, sweetheart," he said. "It'll have to be a modest ring at this point. But maybe the day will come when through my own diligence and efforts I'll be a man of means and I'll replace it with something much, much better."

"Perhaps," said Carli, who hoped that together, united in faith, values, and work ethics, they would provide wonderfully for a family. "But I know a fancy ring would never be as dear to me as the one we'll get today. And even if we do go on to become financially secure in life, it seems kind of sad to think about replacing it simply for something more impressive."

"That's what I love about you, Carli. You're a sweet, unsophisticated, old-fashioned girl. You couldn't be a gold-digging, social-climbing, name-dropping sophisticate if you were ordered to do it. . . !"

Carli laughed at the idea. "I wouldn't have a clue where to even start."

"That's what I like about the influence of small-town, grassroots, rural American living, where your value as an individual person is important, not what you have or who you are. . ."

two

No sooner had the youth group members begun to arrive in the Fellowship Hall, a modern structure built adjacent to the older church building, than a sharp-eyed sophomore, pretty, dark-haired Kirin Arunson grasped Carli's left hand.

"What's this?" She cried in excitement, her eyes twinkling.

"A diamond."

"When did this happen?" the girl exclaimed.

Still feeling almost dazed by the day's events, Carli studied the ring just as the teenagers were doing. Her heart seemed to swell almost to bursting at the witness of its presence. She and Gus, who liked antiques, had found a setting that captured the best of what seemed old-fashioned design with modern style.

"Just this very afternoon," Gus replied.

With Kirin's elated cries regarding the beauty of Carli's ring even more girls who were arriving clustered around to admire the sparkling diamond solitaire in a platinum mounting atop an ornate yellow gold band.

The boys, in a rowdy teenage manner, groaned and teased Gus. Everyone offered congratulations and hinted that they hoped to be invited to the wedding and that it would be held at Old Union Christian Church, even though neither Gus nor Carli were natives of the area.

"Pastor Meyer has the final say on some details," Gus said, smiling at the stocky, bearded preacher who'd stepped into the area to see what the commotion was all about.

"I'd consider it an honor to hear your vows," he said, clapping Gus on the shoulder and giving Carli a quick hug of congratulation, "and at Old Union you're always among friends and church family."

No one had really noticed during the excitement as everyone clustered around the chaperones that Kathie Arunson,

Kirin's older sister, had slipped away to the church office to use the telephone.

Presently the pizza arrived as they were finishing up their Bible study lesson for the evening. The delivery person was one of Gus's employees and had worked with various church youth on scheduled shift teams at the pizzeria. Jerry Morgan came in balancing several red insulated pizza transport bags, returning to his vehicle for more.

Everyone was so busy laying out the aromatic pies that they didn't notice that Kathie Arunson accompanied Jerry to his van with money in hand. They didn't notice her slip into the furnace room that also served as a storage area, before accepting a pizza container from Jerry, and returning to the meeting.

An hour later, after the pizzas had become history, but before the youngsters could begin to think about departing for home, the Arunson sisters retrieved a beautifully decorated cake from the furnace area. Nestled among the ornate lavender, pink, and blue flowers and fluffy ribbons of buttercream trim was *Congratulations Gus & Carli* scripted in frosting.

"Come cut the cake, Gus and Carli! We figured you'd need some practice before you're ready to slice wedding cake on the big day!"

Carli was almost moved to tears.

"A cake! How did you—?" she gasped. "Until this afternoon we didn't even—"

Kathie grinned. "I sneaked away and phoned Jerry and told him the good news. I asked if he'd do us a favor and pick up a deli cake at the supermarket if I called and made arrangements so one of the cakes would be personalized by the time he arrived."

Carli shook her head, amazed at such sweet thoughtfulness. "You little schemer!" Carli said, hugging the girl. "Thanks so much!"

"I thought it'd be fun. Like an engagement party."

"And it is," Carli said. "I never dreamed I'd have one. Maybe it's not like engagement parties wealthy people have, where they plan months in advance to make the announcement on a festive official occasion. But it's just right for us—isn't it, Gus?"

Gus gave an agreeable nod, but seemed distant, and said nothing, as if her words seemed to take him to a different place and time, where mystery memories prevented him from being fully present at that exact moment.

Carli felt herself about to frown, as she did at times, and checked the expression, although inwardly she felt consternation as she had before—on those rare occasions when something someone said seemed to cause Gus to detach from his surroundings. It was almost as if he isolated himself, safe within an invisible cocoon, so immune to what was going on around him that it was as if he were struck emotionless. . . without feeling.

"There's a lot of cake here!" Kathie pointed out. "Why don't you kids who have parents picking you up go invite them in for cake and coffee?"

"Sounds good!" Gus regained his composure and heartily agreed.

Within minutes, their church friends were trouping into the fellowship hall, everyone remarking at once about the surprise of it and the thoughtfulness of the children.

Men were shaking Gus's hand and their wives were giving Carli happy hugs and admiring her ring.

Pastor Meyer fetched his wife and family from the nearby parsonage and they joined the celebration.

"We'll set up an appointment to finalize details," he assured as he took his family in tow, carrying their toddler who was tired and seemed about to nod off to sleep.

"Terrific!" Gus agreed. "I'll be in touch."

Several of the parents looked around at the party clutter.

"Y'all go on home," Carli said, sensing their thoughts. "Gus and I will tidy up the Fellowship Hall."

A few made token protests.

But Carli was adamant.

"Your kids have school tomorrow," Carli pointed out. "Really, it's no trouble."

"None at all," Gus echoed. "Anything that gives us an opportunity to be together is fun for us!"

"Keep that attitude, buddy," one of the long-married men said, laughing, as he gave Gus a fond, playful punch on the upper arm. "That's the spirit!"

"He'll be a good husband, Carli," one of the wives assured.

"Of course," Carli said. "That's why I'm marrying him. He's handsome, hardworking, kind, gentle, thoughtful. . . decent, dedicated, disciplined, determined, devout. . .the list just goes on and on!"

"Lists!" the Arunson girls' father groaned. "Uh-oh, Gus! Carli's a list maker. Watch out—I can assure you that there's a 'Honey Do' list in your future."

"I can hardly wait," Gus said. "And I won't wait—very long."

"Then you'd better be making an appointment with Pastor Meyer," Carli teased, "Just as soon as he arrives in the office tomorrow morning."

"Uh-oh, Gus—she's already giving orders!" the men chuckled.

"That's okay. When it comes to Carli—her wish is my command," Gus affirmed.

As Gus and Carli swept the meeting hall, wiped the tables and countertops, and tied the trash bags and carried them to the dumpster, they discussed their plans for the future. They reached easy decisions. Since the moment they'd met it seemed that they'd shared so much, including likes and dislikes, sharing views and drawing joy from the same simple things in life.

They both loved poking through used bookstores. They liked spending days circulating through the crowds and examining wares at flea markets within easy driving distance on their days off. They enjoyed stopping at quaint antique shops that were common in the area. They didn't make frequent nor expensive purchases. They simply enjoyed talking with the owners, learning bits of local history, and examining artifacts of daily living in eras long gone.

During those times Carli had frequently been reminded that there was a Gus Dennis she didn't know, that he was a man, sometimes reticent, who possessed many talents and abilities, so many of them unknown to her until she witnessed him in action.

Once at an antique store, an establishment that seemed to cater to higher ticket clientele, Gus had admired the displays of fine china. To Carli's surprise, he'd known the various Limoges patterns, and also was familiar with patterns and silvermakers who had long ago produced the gleaming sets of sterling silver flatware encased in beautiful wooden, velvet-lined storage cases.

The proprietor had shown Gus an unusually elegant, but unmarked sterling silver candelabra, which she believed to be from the Revolutionary War period, and the elderly woman and Gus had enjoyed a spirited conversation—discussing pros and cons—as they tried to attribute what seemed an actually unattributable piece of silver work created by an obvious artisan.

The few times they'd played Trivial Pursuit, everyone groaned when they came up against Gus, because his knowledge of esoteric facts and details seemed to place him in a whole different educational stratosphere.

"How can one individual be so well-rounded and knowledgeable about everything?" one of his buddy's once inquired after being severely outclassed during the game.

Gus shrugged. "I read a lot. . ." he offered.

But then he had become detached and emotionless so that it somehow seemed to put a damper on the rest of what had been such a fun and relaxing evening.

With the church folks, it seemed as if Gus could talk to anyone about anything. Whatever topic was of interest to them, Gus could handle his own. Just that very evening he had been talking very deeply with one of the Youth Fellowship member's father who was a stockbroker. Carli herself knew that Wall Street was important in the world of stocks, bonds, and trading, but she didn't begin to understand its inner workings. Somehow Gus did. But she knew that *The*

Wall Street Journal wasn't on his preferred reading list when he regularly visited the public library, although she concluded that he must at least occasionally flip through its pages.

As the newly engaged couple moved about bringing order to the Fellowship Hall, they laughed, joked, and made happy plans for a future together. By evening's end, so much had been settled. They'd decided that Gus would give notice regarding his apartment, and they'd make Carli's place their dwelling. They'd chosen where they'd like to honeymoon; sketched in what they'd hoped to do with their lives.

There was only one area where Gus was withdrawn, and where Carli wasn't allowed to offer input regarding his decisions and choices in life, where communications were dismal, where positive emotions were absent—his past and his family.

Carli was without family by circumstances.

Gus Dennis was without family by choice.

As nice and easygoing as Gus was, Carli wondered just how troublesome his people were that he wanted nothing to do with them, considering his church brothers and sisters the family he'd chosen, the only kin that mattered, the only family he wanted. It wasn't normal, Carli knew, and the situation made her uneasy.

Carli's uneasiness deepened that night when she sat down to pen a note to her elderly, unmarried aunts, Eula Mae and Fanchon, at the rest home where they resided in Tennessee.

As she wrote her happy news, memories took Carli back to times when she was a small girl and after Sunday services her aunts would come for dinner, then stay to sip iced tea and converse the afternoon away. Often they'd commented about area events and people, which included various relationships and unions in the old Kentucky home area.

Although Carli had been too young to appreciate the depth of meaning to the words that were spoken, she'd remembered them and how so frequently they'd summed up a situation with one succinct phrase.

"A person marries an individual—but the entire family's thrown in for free!"

And:

"The fruit doesn't fall far from the tree, y'know!"

Or:

"You can pick a banjo, you can pick a passel of berries, but you sure can't pick your family."

More wisdom of the hills returned to haunt Carli's thoughts long after Gus had dropped her off following their return from the meeting.

The pull of blood could be defied, her mother and old-maid aunts had pointed out, but they'd also seemed to believe that it couldn't be forever denied. There came a time when no matter what family had once been, the call of blood was strong to return to the fold, even if it was like going back to a crime scene.

Was she a fool to marry Gus, who she knew only to the depth that he was emotionally able to allow her entrance into his life? Was she being naive to dare to trust in him as she knew it would be imperative that she commit to a husband when his people, who were bone of his bone, blood of his blood, remained a shadowy secret to be kept from her?

While it was Gus's choice, Carli realized, deep in her heart of hearts she prayed that there could be a reconciliation, a transformation, so that one day Gus Dennis's family would come to know and appreciate him for the person Carli knew her beloved to be. And it was a new prayer that would be unceasing in her heart.

After all, there were many, many scriptures that addressed family dynamics, behavior God espoused for parents. . .and children.

three

Weeks flew by as Carli and Gus were kept busy with their jobs, wedding plans, and shopping for household items that they would need, often finding bargains at thrift stores.

They set their wedding date for the long weekend for the Fourth of July to accommodate their beach honeymoon. Gus scheduled time off from the pizzeria, as Carli did from the insurance company where she worked.

Finally their big day came.

They'd planned a plain but meaningful ceremony with a reception to follow in the church Fellowship Hall. Carli had sent her aunts invitations, even though she knew that ill health would prevent them from attending. Getting sweet letters from them both, wishing her well, had at least given her a sense of being connected to what family ties she still possessed.

The day dawned hazy, with a promise for glorious weather, not too hot, but balmy with a pleasant, cooling breeze.

Carli had found the perfect dress, street length, lacy, and elegant, with a scooped neck, balloon chiffon sleeves, fitted bodice and bell skirt. With her white satin shoes and her mother's pearl necklace, her hazel eyes carefully made up and seeming almost almond shaped, and her creamy, tawny skin, contrasting with her thick, dark, naturally wavy hair, she knew that she had never looked more attractive.

When she put the short veil in place, her features seemed misty and ethereal. For a moment, she wished that they could've had a professional photographer recording these touches. But one of their friends who owned a decent camera had offered to do the honors and for that they were both grateful, for as they all joked, "The price was right."

Carli heard Gus pull up out front. She consulted the mirror one last time, then picked up her white leather Bible, which her parents had given her when she was in high school. It was adorned with a spray of baby's breath and miniature red roses, artfully arranged and affixed to the Bible by a florist's employee who was also a Sunday School teacher at Old Union Christian Church.

Gus was halfway up the sidewalk to the lobby of the apartment house when Carli met him.

"I'm ready!"

He stopped in his tracks, seemingly stunned.

"You're beautiful. Absolutely gorgeous!"

Carli grinned. "You look rather dashing yourself, kind sir," she informed him.

He gallantly offered her his arm. "Shall we go, m'lady?"

"Get me to the church on time!" Carli gaily sang like Eliza Doolittle's reformed father had done in "My Fair Lady."

Once Gus had tucked Carli into his car, it only took a few minutes before they parked in the shade of a big elm tree in front of the church. Already there were a few vehicles in the parking lot.

Carli felt her heart skip a beat with a pulse of nervousness, but soon Pastor Meyer was there to warmly encourage her along and to advise Gus on where to go to be with his groomsman.

There were discreet whispers as Carli and Gus stepped into the narthex in the company of Pastor Rollie. Members of their church family smiled approval, a few winked, and others beamed with pride upon the young couple.

An instant later, Carli was startled when an elderly woman, bent with age, a dowager who reminded Carli of her aunts, leaning upon her cane, exclaimed in a creaky voice that seemed to carry an echo throughout the church sanctuary.

"Don't you know that it's bad luck for a groom to see his bride before their wedding, girl?"

The thump of her cane as she took another step seemed to punctuate the demand.

"Now, Mama. . ." her embarrassed son and daughter-in-law said and tried to shush her as they gave Carli apologetic smiles.

Carli smiled back, but her expression felt wooden, and she was shaken.

At that moment, she felt very alone, and very much aware that she had no family, no father figure to walk her down the aisle and give her away to the man she loved, the man chosen for her by the Lord.

She knew that the wedding was going to be beautiful, what she and Gus wanted. . .but, if only. . .

Carli refused to let herself think of the people she wished could be there with her, and contented herself they were watching from on high, before she forced her thoughts to other topics to stem the quick rush of tears whose source could've been either joy or sad longing.

It seemed only a moment later when the organist thundered into "The Wedding March." Carli's bridesmaid, Marissa, a choir member who'd become a best friend as well as coworker at the insurance company, began to move up the aisle following Pastor Meyer's little girl, Chastity, who was serving as flower girl, while their little boy was Gus's ring bearer.

Then Carli began her walk down the aisle, affixing her eyes firmly on her beloved, her solid yet mysterious husband-to-be.

When Carli joined Gus at the altar, Pastor Meyer cleared his throat as the strains of the organ faded away.

"Dearly beloved," he began, "We are gathered here today. . ."

Raptly Carli listened to the beautiful words of the marriage ceremony, so aware of Gus's strong hand clasping hers as they vowed to forsake all others, taking one another for better or for worse, in sickness and in health. . .for richer or for poorer, until death parted them.

"I do. . ." said Carli.

"I certainly do!" echoed Gus.

"With the power vested in me, I now pronounce you man and wife," Pastor Meyer said. Then he faced the congregation. "May I present to you Mr. and Mrs. Austin J. Dennis III."

There were smiles, rippling murmurs of approval, and then, after Gus chastely kissed Carli, the organist played an even more vibrant rendition of "The Wedding March" as they departed the altar and formed a receiving line in the narthex of the church.

"As good as things are now," a friend teased Gus and Carli, "may they become even better. May you keep your good health and be spared sickness. And if you're feeling poor now. . .just wait until you have kids! And remember that not all forms of 'riches' can be deposited in the bank!"

Those nearby laughed, and as flashes went off, picture takers captured the happy moments for all time.

Soon everyone adjourned to the Fellowship Hall where the ornate wedding cake was the focal point of a long table. The Arunson girls were at the punch bowl on one end, and Pastor Meyer's wife was at the coffeepot as Carli and Gus prepared to cut the elaborate cake that others would serve.

"Any regrets?" Gus whispered when he and Carli were seated.

"None!" she said, smiling.

"Expectations?" He teased.

"More than a few," she whispered and squeezed his hand. "I'll look forward to fulfilling them all!"

Less than an hour later, after detaching her flowers and throwing the bouquet, which was caught by Marissa, the couple ducked to rush through a shower of rice to escape into Gus's car.

Somehow, at some time, some of the teenagers had managed to slip away and tie old cans and boots to drag behind the car that was a riot of white shoe polish and streamers accentuating the *JUST MARRIED!* signs.

Eager to get away on their honeymoon, Carli and Gus changed into casual clothes in record time, removed the paraphernalia from the car, stowed luggage that was already packed and waiting and headed east toward the Atlantic Ocean and the beachfront hotel where they had reservations.

In what seemed no time at all Gus was signing the register, Mr. & Mrs. Austin J. Dennis III, and they began what they dreamed would be the rest of their lives, blissfully, happily, together for always. . . .

ॐ

Upon their return, life settled into a comfortable routine for the newlyweds.

Carli was awarded a promotion at work, and Gus was able to arrange his managerial schedule to allow them more time together, time which they spent poking around at antique shops, attending bluegrass music festivals, or at the church practicing for duets that they frequently sang on Sundays.

Sometimes they sang while doing dishes in their apartment, but kept their voices down to avoid risking disturbing their neighbors.

Autumn was in the air. Carli was busy baking and making crafts for the annual women's group bazaar that was to be held the following weekend. Gus and several of the men had made plans to set up the tables following choir practice after Wednesday night church services so that the room would be ready for the members of the ladies' circle to do the finishing touches for the holiday bazaar.

Carli caught a ride home with another wife while the husbands remained behind to move tables around. Gus seemed troubled when he returned home.

"What's up?" Carli inquired. "You look a bit down."

"Bad news," he sighed. "Reverend Rollie had a heating technician come to check on the furnace today. The diagnosis isn't good."

"They had trouble with it all of last winter."

"This winter it's shot."

Carli winced. "That shoots a hole in the church budget."

"Tell me about it," Gus sighed.

"Times like this. . .I sometimes wish we *were* wealthy," Carli said, "so we could simply write a check for a new furnace and be done with it."

Gus looked at her.

"Would you like to?" He inquired. "Amen to that."

Carli gave an outright laugh. "Of course I'd love to. But I don't think our banker would like it, Gus. Not one bit."

"The Lord will provide," he said. "We must have faith."

And to Carli's amazement, and that of the entire congregation, two weeks later, there was a cashier's check, made out to Old Union Christian Church, in the amount of ten thousand dollars, to purchase and have installed a new furnace system donated by a secretive benefactor who wished to remain anonymous.

"I wonder what wonderful person did that?" Carli mused as they drove home from the services where a radiant Pastor Meyer had made the announcement.

"It doesn't matter who," Gus said, "only that it was done."

"I'm just curious, is all," Carli said. "Most of the people in our home church are about like we are, Gus. Working people trying to make ends meet."

"Maybe it was a philanthropist who got wind of the church's need," he suggested. "Or maybe someone connected to the congregation has rich friends somewhere."

"Or a miracle," Carli said.

Gus grinned and hugged her. "I like that explanation best!"

Carli and Gus had a wonderful Thanksgiving. The church had planned a meal and afternoon for those who wanted to be with their family of faith. A light snow, uncharacteristic in the region, was falling as they walked the few blocks toward their apartment, admiring the Christmas lights that were softly glowing in the dusk.

"I'll have to get going on Christmas cards," Carli said, "and—"

Before Carli could ask if there were any people beside their friends from his Navy days he wished included on the list, Gus seemed to deflect any potential question.

"It'll be a busy time," Gus said, and mentioned that already they had advance orders for various seasonal parties where pizzas were to be served.

"I guess we'll have a quiet Christmas by ourselves."

"It'll be nice," Gus assured.

"I'm especially looking forward to going caroling with the youth group."

"Me, too," Gus admitted.

"We sing well together, you know," Carli said.

"You're way better than I am, Carli. You're good enough to go professional. At least that's my opinion. But we do make beautiful music together."

Carli slipped into his arms and gave his winter-chilled

cheeks a warm kiss. Snowflakes clung to her dark lashes as she smiled up at him.

"In more ways than one," she teased.

"I'll sing harmony with you anytime, Carli Waggoner Dennis!"

By the time they arrived home, the snow was falling more heavily.

"As sticky as the snow is, it'd be just right for making a snowman if a few more inches fall," Carli said.

"If there's nothing good on television tonight, we know what we can do."

"Even if there is something good to watch, making a snowman can take precedence. I might even bundle up and make a snow angel."

Gus brushed at the glittering white crystals that clung to Carli's raven dark curly hair. "You are my snow angel, Caroline, come into my life to thaw my very heart."

four

The day after Thanksgiving, Carli didn't have to go to work because the insurance office had closed for a long weekend. She slept late then rose to catch up on some laundry and cleaning chores.

Later in the afternoon she prepared some Christmas cards to go out and decided to walk them to the postal drop box two blocks away. The air would have been balmy, but there was an icy chill lent by the inches of snow that were melting and settling. The snowman that had been so perfect the night before, and earlier that morning when Gus had left for work, had suffered the ill effects of the warmer temperature combined with sunshine, and instead of proudly waving at the passersby. . .he drooped.

Carli wished that she'd taken a picture that they might have a memento of the first snowman they'd created together.

But even that happy event had a slightly dark shadow cast upon it. When they'd placed the carrot nose in place, and balanced a hat upon its head and secured the scarf around its neck, Carli had teasingly inquired, "Okay, now what do we name him, Gus?"

He gave a shrug. "Anything but Austin IV!"

"He must look like your side of the family," Carli ventured to suggest, "for there's no resemblance to mine!"

Carli used that as an opening gambit, hoping that with the holidays upon them, perhaps it could help to convince Gus to talk about his family, at least describe them to her, for she didn't believe that he even had family photos secreted away in his wallet.

But Gus began whistling to fill the silence surrounding them and making tiny snow applications of adjustment—that the snowman really didn't need.

"I'm getting cold," a suddenly bleak Carli said. "I'm going in."

"Be with you in a moment," Gus said. "Have we got any hot chocolate mix, honey?"

Carli forced a smile. "Coming right up!"

⁂

As Carli stepped outdoors to head toward the postal drop box to be sure to mail the cards before the scheduled evening pickup, she bundled against the chilly breeze. She considered borrowing the old woolen scarf that they'd used to finish the snowman's attire, but realized that it'd be damp and cold, so she settled on simply buttoning her collar more securely around her throat and she'd retrieve the scarf on her way back into the apartment.

About halfway down the block in front of their apartment complex, she spotted a rental car parked beside the curb. Before she could get a good look at the driver, a newspaper was unfolded with a flourish and the gentleman's features were all but hidden behind a copy of *The Wall Street Journal.*

Carli didn't give it much thought when the vehicle was still parked there upon her return from the drop box. She concluded that the fellow either had business with someone in one of the apartments in the complexes that lined both sides of the well-maintained boulevard, or was waiting for someone who did.

An hour later when she went outside to collect the scarf and hat from the snowman that was melted down into his base, she saw that the man was still there. But before she could get a solid look at him, except to know that he was elderly, and seemed kind-faced, a copy of *USA Today* snapped into place.

Carli put the car and its waiting driver from her mind. But as dusk was draping and the city streetlights were coming on to cast a silvery sheen over the remaining bits of snowy landscape, she saw that the car was still there, its engine running, for a stream of exhaust unfurled from the exhaust pipe.

Undoubtedly the fellow had had to run the engine numerous times during the afternoon to warm the vehicle. The situation began to disturb her, and she found herself helpless not to sift through possible explanations for his presence.

Was he a private investigator spying on someone? Actually, she concluded that he hardly looked the part, and if he was, then he had a bit to learn about unobtrusive surveillance, for he'd certainly not tried to hide the fact of his presence.

Was he lost?

Was he merely confused? Many times Carli had heard reports on newscasts about some elderly person, suffering with Alzheimer's, who'd slipped away from sheltered care and eventually been discovered wandering, or waiting, before someone intervened and they were returned to their worried caretakers.

Was he homeless and living in a rental car because he couldn't afford both the agency fees and the price of a place to stay?

Carli realized that there didn't seem to be anything ominous nor threatening about his very presence. But as minutes passed she felt a strong need to intervene, but just couldn't quite bring herself to do so for fear of looking the fool.

"Carli Dennis, you have read entirely too many detective novels and watched more television than is good for your overactive imagination," she chided herself as she turned away, assuring herself that the next time she looked he'd be gone.

But fifteen minutes later when she peeked out, the vehicle was still there.

She wished that Gus were there; he was good about this kind of thing, and he wouldn't know the tingle of fear that she experienced at the thought of tossing on a coat and gloves and going out to ask a complete stranger what he was doing parked in front of their complex all afternoon. There were "Neighborhood Watch" stickers in many of the windows in the various complexes, but if the neighborhood had been watching, apparently they hadn't found the old gentleman too threatening to their environment.

Finally, Carli slipped into her coat, smoothed on gloves, then exited the apartment by the back entrance, skirted the side of the building, cut across the damp, spongy lawn and approached the rental agency vehicle from the rear, coming up on the driver's side.

She pecked on the window.

The gentleman who'd been reading, with the use of a small penlight, almost jumped out of his skin at the unexpected noise.

He pressed a button and the window slid down.

"I couldn't help noticing that you've been parked here all afternoon," Carli blurted. "Are you lost? May I help you?"

Before the startled man could answer, Carli saw that *The Wall Street Journal* and *USA Today* had been neatly folded and placed on the passenger side, and it was a well-worn Bible that the old man had been reading with the aid of a small flashlight. She felt a rush of commonality with him, a trust that was instinctive when dealing with others whom she recognized as believers.

"Actually, Miss, I'm waiting for someone to arrive home. An old friend. I'd been told that this was where he lived. Maybe my source was incorrect."

"I know most of the people in the apartment house," Carli said. "Who are you looking for?"

"Austin Dennis. . .do you know him? Does he live here?"

For a moment Carli felt weak-kneed. "Yes. . .he does. . .we do. . .I'm his wife."

The old gentleman looked truly pleased and gave Carli a sweet, delighted smile. "Praise God, I was hoping that Gussie would find himself, discover happiness, and—"

Somehow Carli didn't think the fellow could be Gus's father. But she knew that there was some connection.

"You must be frozen—and tired of sitting here," she said. "I'm Carli Dennis," she introduced. "Gus and I got married last summer. Would you like to come in and warm up and wait for Gus?"

"If you're sure it's no trouble."

"None at all," Carli said.

"Jasper Winthrop's the name, Mrs. Dennis. I'm retired now, but I've known Gus since he was a little boy. I decided I'd like to see him again while there's still time. . ."

"Come right this way," Carli invited.

Minutes later, Jasper Winthrop was comfortably established in the Dennis kitchenette savoring a hot cup of coffee and the sandwich that Carli had prepared.

He brimmed with questions about Gus, most of which Carli could answer, and she realized she was dying to pose questions of her own, which she suspected Jasper Winthrop could explain to her satisfaction.

Did she dare do so? she wondered, for it seemed almost like a betrayal of Gus's need for privacy to investigate the past which he preferred not to speak about.

"What kind of business do you have with Gus?" Carli finally ventured to ask.

Mr. Winthrop hesitated. "Actually, no offense, Mrs. Dennis, but that's something I'd rather wait and discuss with Gus. . ."

Feeling that she and the elderly man had about exhausted neutral topics, Carli arose and announced that she was going to call Gus and see if he could come home early.

Presently he was on the line. She was grateful that Mr. Winthrop had excused himself to go to the lavatory to wash up after eating so that she had some privacy.

"What's up, Carli?"

"Gus. . .I know that this is going to sound silly, but there was a car parked on the street all afternoon. It was there for the past four or five hours with an older man sitting in it. It's like he was waiting for someone. . .I thought perhaps he was lost." She lowered her voice, "You know, like one of those Alzheimer patients who wanders away?"

Gus gave an amused laugh. "So Angel of Mercy Carli has him safely in the apartment, right? Tell you what, honey, call the police. They'll know what to do. I'll come home early."

"The man's not confused, Gus," Carli said. Then she took a deep breath. "It turns out that this fellow, Jasper Winthrop, was waiting for you to come home."

Instead of chuckling and teasing her about an overactive imagination and her do-gooder behavior, Gus gave a tight sigh. He seemed barely able to restrain a disgusted oath.

"Good old Uncle Jasper. . .I was afraid it'd come to this."

"Gus—what's wrong?"

"I guess the game's up," he sighed tiredly. "Somehow I always knew it would come to this."

"Gus—are you in trouble?!" Carli cried, her throat clenching with fear as she considered the unbelievable.

"No. . .no more than usual. But, perhaps you are, Carli."

Carli felt an icy, slashing sensation at the same instant her words burst from her. "What do you mean. . . ?"

"My family, Carli dear, has finally decided to contact me. . ."

"Is that so bad?"

"The past being what it is, I doubt that it'll be good."

"Gus, you need to face your past. My own father did. Others have. You should, too!"

"I don't want to ever go back to my past. Not even to face it."

"Why?"

"Because those who return to the past too often learn that they have no futures!"

"Gus, you're confusing me."

"Haven't you figured it out yet, Carli?" Gus quietly asked. "I don't have a family, Carli, what I have is Dennis Mining and Manufacturing! People think that our family owns it—but the unvarnished truth is—that the corporation owns us!"

"Oh. . .heavens!" For a moment Carli couldn't even think. Dennis was a common enough name that she wouldn't have the made connection in her wildest dreams, for such a possibility would've seemed not only remote but downright laughable.

"We took each other for better or worse, in sickness and in health, for richer and poorer. Right?"

"Yes."

"You thought you married a blue-collar working fellow, correct."

"Yes."

"You did. . .and you didn't. I happen to be a working stiff who was born with a huge trust fund in his name. I tapped into those funds and bought the church its new heating system out of what my family considers pocket change."

"Oh. . .Gus!"

"I was hoping that after having ignored it all for so long no one would notice. But they were probably waiting for me to make just such a move."

Suddenly, so many little things, casual comments, throwaway remarks made glaring, unmistakable sense. In his own way Gus had been casting hints, paving the way for the moment of truth. . .to better prepare her, should it ever come to. . .this.

"Carli?. . .Whatever happens. Please remember that I'll always love you. Always and forever."

"Yes, Gus," Carli whispered, even as in her heart, she felt helpless not to doubt him.

If he loved her so fully and so faithfully, why had he withheld from her basic truths about himself and his station in life?

Before he hung up, Carli sensed that Gus actually might be feeling relieved that the truth was out.

But for her part, she was feeling more and more grieved. Why had he not trusted her sufficiently to tell her the entire truth, and trust that she'd want what he wanted, respect his choice, be content that he'd turned his back on wealth and the world? Once again she felt a stab of anger that Gus could be so unfeeling and detached that he'd acted as if she didn't have emotions and feelings, too. And worst was the ugly idea that Gus had been manipulating and controlling her in the ways that it seemed he'd most resented his family having done to him.

Helplessly, Carli began to cry.

A moment later she felt a warm and comforting hand on her shoulder, and a gentle touch smoothing her hair as her father had done when minor things had seemed to break her heart when she was a child.

"These hard times will end, Carli," Jasper whispered. "After all, it says in the Good Book, 'And it came to pass'. It's never said, 'And it came to stay forever.' This has a beginning, and it'll have an end. The Lord uses us as He will to execute His perfect plans for us. You're going to be caught in the middle of much unpleasantness, my dear," he predicted, "and my old heart grieves for that. But I know that the Lord loves you, and everyone involved, and He won't allow it to go on for one more moment than necessary to work transforming changes in those who need to turn away from their erroneous ways."

What the kindly old gent said in his New England Yankee accent, so echoed what her father would've counseled in his soft twanging drawl, that Carli felt a rush of affection for the old Dennis family friend, and laid her soft, smooth hand over his gnarled with age.

"I know—" she sniffed.

"Gus's father has found his peace with the Lord," Jasper Winthrop shared. "But 'tis no doubt his mother that'll be pursued as if by the Hound of Heaven. And she—that woman will be a tough nut to crack before she gives way and gives herself to the Lord."

"My daddy had a saying about folks like that," Carli said. "He used to claim that they were 'Struck right tight to the griddle' and that it took a lot of careful prying to get them ready to be turned over intact."

Jasper Winthrop gave a rich laugh. "You're a godsend, Carli Dennis. Perhaps the one woman in the entire world who can go up against Mitzi Dennis. . .and live to know the glory of it all. Gus needs you but I think Mitzi needs you more. She's a sad, and seeking, sorrowing woman, so caught up in her worldly ways that she hasn't the time nor inclination to know what it is that she's even feeling, and to open up to the fact that the Lord Jesus Christ is the healing balm her tortured soul desires."

five

Carli and Jasper Winthrop sat in a strained stillness that soon became an easy silence as they waited for Gus to arrive home. The silence wasn't uncomfortable any longer, Carli realized, because they were both in prayer. She knew she certainly was!

The air of expectation created an almost prestorm calm atmosphere in the apartment. Jasper and Carli's eyes flew up to meet in a locked, uncertain gaze when they heard the door of Gus's car slam shut. Carli felt frozen.

Ordinarily she would have met Gus at the door. But this time, with the thoughts and emotions that had been filling her, Carli felt leaden beneath the weight of it all and realized that she was so unsure of what Gus's basic reaction would be that it was as if she were waiting for the other shoe to drop.

Apparently Jasper Winthrop felt no such hesitation. With a wheeze he boosted himself from the sofa and was just inside the doorway as Gus unlocked it.

At the sight of Jasper, Gus stopped in his tracks. A seeming kaleidoscope of emotions seemed to ripple across his features.

"Gus, my boy!" Mr. Winthrop took the initiative. He clasped Gus in a bear hug that the younger man was helpless not to respond to with a return hug of his own. Carli noticed that Gus squeezed his eyes tightly shut to stem tears of emotion provoked by the presence of the old family friend who'd obviously meant much to him at one time.

"You're looking well, Gus," Jasper said. "And what a wonderful, wonderful girl you've taken for your wife."

"She's a pearl," Gus said, then went to Carli, helped her from her chair and put his arm around her. "It's been years, Uncle Jasper, but you haven't changed a bit."

"Maybe not where it shows. But, I'm older, wiser. . .and a

born-again Christian now, Gus, as I discover you and your dear wife both are, too."

Gus nodded. "So what are you doing these days, Uncle Jasper. Surely you're retired by now?"

"I was your grandfather's aide, and then your father's right-hand man. I did retire, but I've left retirement—briefly, I hope—to help my old friends, the Dennis family."

"I see. . ." Gus said, even though to Carli, it was clear that Gus did not see. And neither did she.

"Your father needs you, Gus," Jasper quietly said.

Gus gave a bitter, rueful laugh.

"He's never needed anything or anyone except his work. . . work. . .WORK!"

Jasper didn't disagree. "That's no longer true, son, thank God. Your father's a changed man. I found the Lord some years ago and it was to my great joy that I was able to lead your father to the Lord. He used to be a driven man, Gus, and mercilessly drove those around him to excel. But he's been a man at peace for several years now."

Gus said nothing. Carli didn't know if he wouldn't speak, out of the old hurt and stubbornness from the past, or if he couldn't speak for fear of dissolving into heart-wrenching sobs.

"He's missed you terribly, Gus," Jasper said softly. "But he made no attempt to locate you. . .as he could quite easily have done by following a paper trail left by you. . .but he felt that he had no right to intervene in your life if at last you'd found happiness away from your family and the corporate firm."

Gus swallowed hard and nodded.

"But the truth is, Gus, that your father would very much like to see you, at least one more time. . .before he. . ." This time Jasper paused. When he regarded the couple there was a sheen that dampened his gaze. "He's not a well man, Gus. He's dying. But he's living in the Lord and he'll die that way, too."

Gus could no longer contain his powerful feelings. He began wiping the tears away, removing one only to have another replace it.

"And Mother?" He gently inquired. "How's she doing?"

Jasper gave a sad shake of his head. "Not well, I'm afraid. She pretends that Austin's going to recover, even though all of the specialists have diagnosed his illness as terminal. She refuses to believe or accept it."

"Mother's never accepted anything she hasn't wanted to accept," Gus said.

"I'm afraid this time Mitzi will have to," Jasper said. "The Dennis money is worthless now, and so are her political and social connections. She could be spending quality time with the husband who loves her so. . .but instead she's frantically contacting these newfangled New Age gurus and amassing a rock collection of crystals and smiling and being giddy and vivacious to keep up appearances when those of us close to her are aware that she's paralyzed with feelings of fear, help-lessness and impending loneliness."

"That can't be helping Dad," Gus murmured.

"It's not. We're not sure how much time he has left, Gus. It could be a matter of only a few days, or perhaps even as much as a month. But it won't be long now. Your father has always been concerned about the corporation. You know that."

Gus nodded. "Only too well. . ."

"This time his concern isn't with profit and loss state-ments. Now he cares about the people who've given so much to Dennis Mining and Manufacturing, and, as a result, have caused such rich blessings for the Dennis family."

Jasper seemed to expect Gus to say something, and when he didn't, he continued on.

"Dennis Mining and Manufacturing stock has been one of the Widow's and Orphan's stocks, you know, right up there along with AT&T and Old Blue in stock investment portfo-lios. We've had some rocky times with the economy, but the corporation has remained stable and there was never a need for layoffs, or even downsizing. The firm was loyal to the people who'd been so loyal to it. Your father is concerned what will happen to these people if there isn't a smooth tran-sition of power at Dennis Mining & Manufacturing."

Gus swallowed hard.

"There are corporate raiders, and if your father passed away without a key person in charge to see the firm through a troubled time, Dennis Mining and Manufacturing could face the forces poised to attempt a hostile takeover, or heaven knows what. Corporate raiders are not known for holding sentimental feelings toward the people who labored long and hard to help a company succeed. Your father is concerned that unless a sense of trust is invoked in time stockholders could become squeamish and a corporate entity that was built over the decades could be destroyed in a matter of days, causing great tragedy to countless people across the nation who've believed in Dennis Mining and Manufacturing."

"I can appreciate that," Gus said.

And Carli knew that the way he'd kept up on Wall Street and had an understanding of how the world of big business and high finance worked, that he understood nuances and ramifications that had escaped her, even though she could see the dire potential ahead.

"That's where you come in, Gus," Jasper said.

"Me?" Gus queried, startled.

"You." Jasper cleared his throat.

"But I haven't even been around the family in years. My knowledge of the inner workings of Dennis Mining and Manufacturing seems less than zilch!"

"That doesn't matter, quite frankly," Jasper said. "There are competent and knowledgeable people who'll remain on staff. You can rely on them."

"Then what does anyone need me for?"

"Your name, son," Jasper said. "Austin Dennis III is simply one more fellow in a line bearing the name that people know they can trust."

Gus groaned. "What's in a name?" He inquired bitterly.

Jasper shrugged. "Millions upon millions, on the line, win or lose, depending on how smoothly a transition can be made. I know this is asking a lot of you, Gussie, but please consider it. Not only as a son honoring a father, but as a Christian man caring for the public trust. A lot of persons managing to live careful, comfortable, prudent, financially secure lives could be lost to chaos, trauma, and destitution if you refuse."

Gus dropped his face into his cupped hands. Sensing his anguish, Carli laid a gentle hand on his shoulder.

She thought of her Aunts Eula Mae and Fanchon—and a lot of Americans like them—who'd purchased stocks in companies like Dennis Mining and Manufacturing and desperately counted on the dividends to allow them to live decent and dignified lives.

"What do you think, Carli?" Gus asked. He faced her, his eyes haunted, his expression almost like one dead.

"We'll do whatever you feel that the Lord would have you do, Gus," she said in a simple tone. "I like living here in Virginia, but, like Ruth, I will go where you go. . . The choice is yours, Gus."

"You don't have to decide this very instant," Jasper said. "Think on it. Pray on it. I'd appreciate if you could have some idea of your answer by the morning, however. There's not time to be lost. . ." He stiffly arose, seeming to ease kinks from his spine. "I'll be flying back to Boston tomorrow afternoon."

Gus simply nodded, and Carli could tell he was stunned by all that had happened, everything that lay ahead, circumstances that he simply couldn't, in good conscience, flatly turn his back upon.

"I must be going," Jasper said, and reached for his overcoat and hat on the hall tree.

"Where are you going?" Carli asked.

"Off to find a room for the night," he said.

"You don't have a reservation somewhere?"

"No. I'm afraid I came to this address right away, afraid I'd miss Gus otherwise."

Carli removed the coat from his grip and put it back on the hall tree, along with his hat. "Then you're not going anywhere except into our guest room, Uncle Jasper."

"Oh. . .no. . .I won't interfere—" He started to protest that Carli had already been most accommodating and that he wouldn't take advantage of her sweet nature.

"You're not interfering, and you're not going any farther than your car to collect your overnight case."

"That's right, Uncle Jasper," Gus affirmed, and Carli was grateful to see that he no longer looked like a man who'd been dealt an almost killing blow. "Carli has spoken. And when Carli speaks—everyone had better listen."

"Including E.F. Hutton, I presume?" Jasper made a feeble joke.

Gus shrugged. "If he knows what's good for him. And I know that Dad always held the man in the highest of esteem."

"You will, too, son," Jasper said.

Carli looked from Gus, to Jasper, then back again.

"You're. . .going home. . .then?" she gently questioned.

"A prodigal son is returning to accept a father's blessing."

Carl slipped an encouraging arm around Gus. "Whither thou goest, I, too, shall go. . . ."

"And I'll be there, Lord willing, anytime that either of you should need me," Jasper Winthrop promised.

"If the Lord is with us," Gus said, "who can be against us?"

Jasper thought for a moment, then looked almost ill. "Your mother, for one, and the silly heathen gods she's chosen to worship!"

six

Gus didn't sleep well that night. Carli spent the wee hours tossing and turning, also. The couple didn't speak. Carli sensed that Gus needed to be alone in the dark soul of the night in order to reach his own decisions, form his own conclusions.

Toward dawn they fell asleep, hands still clasped. It was the only way she knew to silently convey to Gus that whatever his choices, she would be supportively at his side.

Carli's eyes felt gritty when she awakened shortly after dawn to fix breakfast for themselves and their guest. Gus wasn't scheduled to go to work until ten, but Carli was expected at the office by nine.

"Breakfast's ready," she summoned Gus and Jasper Winthrop.

After grace, conversation was stilted, but only for a moment, before both men got right to the heart of the matter.

Carli knew that their lives were destined to change, but her mind had been so overloaded with considerations that she'd failed to even give thought to some aspects.

"We'll be leaving for Boston tomorrow at the latest," Gus said, exhaustion tinging his features and his tone. "I'll be giving notice at the pizzeria this morning. You'll need to give notice too, Carli."

For a moment she stared. She realized perhaps it had been naive, but that she'd believed that when the crisis in Boston was passed that they'd return to the niche they'd created for themselves in rural Virginia.

Then she realized that once they departed—very likely, there was no going back. . . .

"I wish we had time to give two weeks' notice," Gus admitted, "but that isn't possible."

"Sometimes we have to accept life on life's terms," Jasper

quietly pointed out. "I'm sure that your employers will understand."

"And even if they don't," Gus said, "what does it really matter? With Dennis Mining and Manufacturing money behind us, what do we need jobs for?" Gus felt for Carli's hand and gave it an encouraging squeeze. "Ready to go to Boston and learn how to be the wife of a CEO, sweetheart?"

Carli took a deep breath. "Just tell me what to do," she quietly replied.

"Just be yourself, dear girl," Jasper assured, "and everyone will absolutely love you. . ."

Carli gave him a fond and grateful smile, hoping that it would be as easy a transition as Uncle Jasper seemed to assume. But in her heart of hearts, she was riddled with doubt.

The day was spent in a whirlwind of activity before Carli and Gus saw Jasper Winthrop off in time for him to drive the rental car back to the terminal in Norfolk for his afternoon flight, knowing that they would be tracing the same path the next day, driving a rental car themselves so that they wouldn't have to worry about long-term parking for their own vehicle.

Carli gave notice, explaining only that there was a medical emergency with Gus's family in the Northeast. She made no further explanations, most certainly not admitting that Gus's family was the Dennis family of wealth and fame. She needed time to adjust to that reality before she tried to explain it to others.

Gus resigned his position at the pizzeria. Then the pair spent the day packing what items couldn't be left behind, and preparing the remainder to be left behind in the apartment that they would continue to rent, even if the premises were used as mere storage for the ragtag assortment of possessions they had accumulated.

"May as well pack light, Carli," Gus said. "We'll both have to go shopping as soon as we hit town. What's appropriate apparel here simply won't do in Boston."

Carli raised an eyebrow, but said nothing.

"There'll be enough tongues wagging about the prodigal

son's returning to the family fold without giving them further ammunition to gossip about. . .with us arriving looking like 'poor relatives.' " Gus seemed not to even notice Carli's stricken look. "If Mother didn't throw out all of my clothes, some of the classic styles will still do for me—but you're in for a completely new wardrobe."

"If that's what we have to do. . .that's what we have to do," Carli said. "I don't want to do anything to. . .embarrass you."

At that moment, more than anything, Carli wanted Gus to take her into his arms, hold her tight, and assure her that he loved her just the way she was and that she could never do anything to embarrass him nor cause him social discomfort. But seeming embroiled in his own considerations, it was as if Gus was blissfully unaware of Carli's emotional needs and feelings.

"Don't worry, sweetheart," Gus said, "you're a quick learner. You'll pick up all the social necessities handily enough. And, I'm sure Mother will do her level best to help you."

"Constructive criticism, I assume?" Carli said in a tone that was a mixture of bleak sarcasm, which Gus totally missed.

"That's the spirit!" he approved, giving her a quick squeeze. "The Lord'll give you strength to deal with Mother."

"From what Uncle Jasper said. . .I'm going to need it."

"Mother's quite a piece of work, I'll admit. But I think you're going to like Dad. Especially now that he's a Christian."

"We'll find out soon enough, won't we, Gus? By this time tomorrow we'll be at his hospital suite."

"It's like we've fallen into some kind of. . .dream. . .from which there's no awakening, isn't it?" Gus mused.

Carli turned away, but did not reply out loud. *Nightmare is more like it!* she thought to herself, for already there were subtle changes in Gus that she realized she didn't like, didn't like at all. She realized that one was a product of his upbringing. Social workers could argue nature versus nurture to their hearts' content, but the bottom line was that in Carli's view, everything that a person had lived through, day by day, year by year, contributed to who that person was as an individual and added up to become traits that could be viewed as good, bad, or indifferent, but nevertheless a person's sum total of behaviors.

There were now aspects of Gus which she was seeing for the first time and realized she didn't particularly like nor admire. Was he seeing the same shortcomings in her?

She knew that the Dennis family would have such expectations for the returning son, the soon-to-be CEO of Dennis Mining and Manufacturing. Would he, in turn, have unrealistic expectations and demands of her? Could she even fulfill them in good conscience?

"Lord," she prayed aloud, and then supplicated quietly within the confines of her heart, *give me the strength to do Your will and to be the Christian helpmate and wife that Gus needs. Let me be a witness to You and protect me from the ways of the world. . .*

Pastor Meyer had been shocked and dismayed to learn that he was going to be missing the Dennises from the choir and church congregation. No one spoke in terms of finality, but he seemed to sense the likelihood that they would not be returning. He shook his head over the irony that it had been Gus's move to tap into trust fund money to purchase Old Union Christian Church a new furnace that had resulted in his family knowing exactly where he was living.

"Our thoughts and prayers for you both will be as warm as the furnace with which you've gifted your church family, Gus. We appreciate that. The Lord sometimes works in very mysterious ways, and we must remember that all things, even tragedies, do work toward good for those who love the Lord. Keep that in mind," he counseled as he hugged them both good-bye as they prepared to go to head for the airport.

For Carli's part, she found that she dwelled on little else, for it helped her to accept the situation to realize that God in His Sovereignty had chosen this path for her, and that she would not be walking unfamiliar byways alone, for the Lord would be with her, guiding her perfectly, if she would only allow Him to lead that she might follow.

Carli had flown a few times in her life, but she'd never

flown first-class, and she felt a bit dismayed when Gus insisted that their seats be upgraded to first-class for the flight to Boston. But she said nothing. She realized that with all of the emotions weighing Gus down he was sometimes focusing on the abstract in order to better ignore the concrete facts.

When they were comfortably settled in, seat belt secured for takeoff, Gus read an airline magazine and Carli let her seat back, closed her eyes and hoped that she could manage to take a nap.

Although she kept her eyes closed and feigned sleep so that the flight attendant didn't disturb her, sleep was far from her as her mind churned. Carli tried to recall what she'd read over the years about the illustrious Dennis family in such diverse places as *People* and headlines shrieking from supermarket tabloids strategically placed at store checkout counters.

Suddenly so many things made almost exquisite sense where they'd seemed simply confusing circumstances previously.

No wonder Gus wanted to know "real people" when his childhood had been spent surrounded by posturing and image-conscious people. Many of those whom he'd grown up with he had recognized as fraudulent personalities, especially those who'd found it necessary to "reinvent" themselves every so often in order to stay viable in the unusual realms where they found their livelihood, such as Hollywood, Las Vegas, and other high-profile areas.

It explained why Gus had enjoyed his well-maintained, but older-model car, and was most content when he was behind the wheel. After all, he'd spent his childhood riding in luxury-model cars, purchased with an eye to impressing others with the family's success, or else in being transported to various culturally stimulating lessons in a chauffeur-driven limousine.

Carli understood why Gus seemed to have basked in the cozy comfort of their small, homey apartment, for he'd been raised in the Dennis Mansion that was more like a museum sheltering priceless "objects d'art" than it was a home. His past gave reason to why he seemed to have liked the apartment complex, close to myriad neighbors, from all walks of life. It was a lifestyle the opposite of what he'd known at the family compound, which, from spreads Carli had seen long ago in magazines very much appeared to rival the Kennedy Compound in Hyannis Port, Massachusetts, for luxury and state-of-the-art security measures.

The regimented past that he had fled explained why Gus enjoyed a flexible go-with-the-flow and serendipitous lifestyle. For too many years he'd lived with the organized pressures of lessons, ranging from violin, to piano, to voice, to skating, horsemanship, and heaven knew what else, until every minute of his life had been scheduled to be socially productive. He'd known few moments of simply enjoying himself as a child, and when he'd attended various outings, he'd been forewarned not to do anything to bring scandal upon the family name, but to always conduct himself in a manner designed to do the Dennis dynasty proud.

Now Carli understood why, when she and Gus had dreamed together of their future, one where they'd hoped to have a house full of children, why Gus was already planning that they'd take fun family vacations and do things together. After all, Austin Dennis III had been relegated to the care of a profusion of nannies, who came and went as they fell out of favor with the regal Mitzi Dennis. And his summers, from the days when he was scarcely more than a toddler, had been spent away from his family at some expensive summer camp where the elite families around the world paid huge sums so their children could become acquainted with the offspring of worldly, powerful children such as themselves. Their hope was that such introductions tracing back to days at summer camp might one day force beneficial alliances in the world of big business and politics.

Gus had a taste for simple, casual, durable, modestly priced clothing, too, while they lived in Virginia. Carli sensed she understood that, too, for he'd no doubt from infancy on been dressed up like a Little Lord Fauntleroy, subjected to tuxedos and dress slacks, ties, and wing-tip shoes when average children his age knew the joys of comfortable jeans, roomy tee-shirts, and less than pristine sneakers. Gus had endured boring, time-consuming sessions with tailors and top-of-the-line haberdashers when other youths had scrambled into Sears and J.C. Penney wear for special occasions.

And debutantes!

Without being told, Carli was aware that Gus could've had his pick from any of the cultured, educated, wealthy, and socially connected young women, whose days were comprised of beauty treatments, shopping, club meetings, and tea parties, born into families as powerful and prestigious as his own. Surely there were socialite mothers who'd encouraged their pampered daughters to set their sights on the goal of wedding Austin Dennis III from playpen days onward.

Defiance, Carli thought, and stole a glance at Gus in the airplane seat next to her. He was reading the in-flight magazine with a seriousness as if he were cramming for a test. And the day's copy of *The Wall Street Journal* that he'd picked up on the run at the Norfolk Airport was awaiting his digestion.

Carli closed her eyes, growing more reflective as she considered what she could assume about Gus's upbringing, and compared it with her own raising. Knowing what she now knew, it made sense and explained a lot of his behaviors and character foibles. A sense of dread had draped over Carli, and she was unable to shake it.

Would she and Gus get along so well. . .or would they get along at all. . .when he returned to his people and the way of life that he'd known for so long?

In Carli's view, it suddenly all seemed to boil down to defiance. She was unable to cast the niggling, disturbing word from her mind. It had been defiance, a form of rebellion, that had motivated Gus to run away from his family, all that he had known, and make a rather anonymous way in the world.

The adult Gus seemed to have lived out his daily life doing everything that his parents would not have considered, and purposely not doing what they would have viewed as normal, responsible social and business protocol.

Did his rebellion even include marrying me? Even though

it might have been a subconscious and very subliminal choice. She knew that gorgeous, Martha—Mitzi—Dennis, who'd lent her name and image to various charitable and philanthropic efforts, some of which Carli had considered questionable, if not outright ridiculous, would not consider a coal-miner's daughter a suitable selection for their only son's mate.

As different as Carli realized they would be. . .would there ever be any winning Gus's family over and finding a place of acceptance in their hearts? She wouldn't have long to wait, she realized, for the flight attendant was instructing them to secure their seat restraints for landing at Logan International Airport.

As they entered Boston's airspace, Gus came to life. He leaned across Carli, pointing out various familiar landmarks of the city she was seeing for the first time. Despite what few remarks he'd made about his long, if unhappy, childhood. . . Carli Dennis knew her husband well enough to realize that he was glad to be home.

For her part, Carli was thankful that kindly Uncle Jasper had promised to meet them at the airport. With a gentle, caring, Christian friend to guide her, somehow Carli knew that whatever transition she was required to make would be much, much easier. . . .

seven

"Well, we're here!" Gus said, collecting Carli's one decent suitcase that they'd tightly packed with the few belongings they were transporting with them. Gus had concluded that his duffel bag from the Navy was simply too ratty to use even though it could have held much more.

Carli gave a weak smile and arose, easing her coat into place, patiently waiting for the other first-class passengers to clear the aisle so that she and Gus could move toward the exit with ease.

"I hope Jasper's waiting at the gate," Carli said.

"He'll be here," Gus said. "He's a man you can count on. What you see is what you get."

"That's reassuring," Carli murmured, trying to shove from mind the unpleasant thought that her husband, Gus Dennis, had seemed to evolve to become more and more someone else with each passing moment as the jet had transported them closer to Boston.

Had it been a mistake to encourage him to confront his past? Had Gus been right that sometimes returning to the past only meant that a future—their future—was jeopardized by such a return to times-gone-by?

Scarcely had they cleared the ramp and the hallway leading into the terminal waiting area, than Gus tensed and barely managed to contain a soft, wretched groan. He seemed to steel himself inwardly as outwardly it was as if a different persona had slipped into place.

"Put on your gloves, Carli!" he ordered under his breath.

"What?"

"Put your gloves on—right now!"

"But—"

"Would you just do it?"

Feeling stung, Carli did as she was told, not understanding, at all, why Gus was insisting that she don gloves, especially now that they were going inside the building, and it hadn't been that nippy in the accordion-walled hallway that had connected the airplane to the terminal.

Looking down, Carli slid the gloves into place. When she glanced up again, she suddenly realized why Gus had begun issuing orders.

Not only was Jasper Winthrop there—but a whole crowd of persons had come to Logan International Airport to welcome the heir to the Dennis fortunes home again.

"This is worse than I'd anticipated," Gus said from behind teeth that were clenched into a radiant, happy smile. "How dare Mother turn this into a media circus event!"

Carli was aware that Gus was seething, but she'd have never guessed it from the perfect smile that was frozen on his handsome features.

"Oh. . .Gus!" Carli's heart was in her throat. She looked up at him, self-conscious, and stricken.

It was as if he had no awareness of her bereft feelings, no appreciation for the whirlpool of strange and frightening emotions within which she felt so trapped and alone, for Gus was so wrapped up in his own moment that it was as if she'd failed to even exist at his side.

"Smile, Carli!" He spat from behind that dazzling smile. "For heaven's sake, the paparazzi are here! Do you want them to print that the Dennis heir and his bride look less than happy together? Do you want the society columnist to start writing snide little innuendoes speculating that there might be marital problems? Do you want—oh, just smile—"

Gus abruptly chopped off further speech when he realized that others would soon be within earshot.

Carli felt on the verge of tears, felt like doing anything but smiling, but she was determined not to embarrass Gus, and she prayed for strength to look happy, composed, and confident. As quaky as her smile felt, and as shaky as her lips, she was unsure that she looked anything but as miserable as she felt.

A moment later Gus was engulfed in hugs and handshakes

all around as photographers' flashes lit up the immediate area like a mini pyrotechnic display.

"Oh. . .you! You awful little vixen!" a gorgeous, heavily scented, longhaired, ravishing girl, who looked a few years older than Carli, pulled the uncomfortable Kentuckian into an embrace, crying shrilly. "You stole my best boyfriend—and married him. Oh. . .I hate you—and I don't even know your name yet—!"

"It's Carli," she spoke, identifying herself, when it seemed Gus was unable to extricate himself from the media personnel's questions in order to make proper introductions.

"What kind of name is Carli? " Mitzi Dennis, whom Carli felt had no room to talk, demanded to know.

"It's my pet name for her, Mother," Gus interceded. "It's short for Caroline. Her name is Caroline Dennis."

He suddenly took Carli's hand and gave it a squeeze, not an encouraging one, but a gesture that she could only interpret as a warning that she had been renamed, and not to dispute the matter.

The attractive auburn-haired woman, gorgeous enough to make her living as a model, or an actress, was all but hanging on Gus.

"Caroline, meet my longtime friend, Lauren Beekman."

"How do you do?" Carli said, and extended her gloved right hand.

While people around them were still chuckling over Lauren's words, Carli realized that the pampered socialite debutante probably didn't really mean it, that she didn't really "hate" Carli, and that it was just the kind of hyperbole people of her ilk used when talking to one another, but it did nothing to bolster Carli's confidence.

Instead of being welcomed. . .the first words she'd heard had been an expression of hatred. Joking, or not, the blithe, heartless remark hurt.

The next thing Carli knew, the girl, Lauren, was tugging at the glove that covered her left hand.

"Let me see your ring!" she squealed, as others clustered close to get their own looks at the stone that the Dennis heir had selected for the beloved that he was finally bringing around his family and friends from the past.

Carli felt as if she wasn't even present, as if they viewed her as a store mannequin and not a human being with feelings and sensitivities as the glove was stripped from her and lost among those clustered about in the noisy crowd with photographers flashing shots inches away from their faces.

There was a horrid hush as her hands, nails unpainted, the modest ring slipped sideways on her finger from the glove's removal, was bared and held aloft for those gathered around to see. A dead silence fell among the fanfare, almost as if they were left speechless, when they confronted the diamond's diminutive size.

At least they didn't laugh, Carli contented herself.

But inwardly, perhaps they were, for poor Gus was blushing as if he'd done something terribly, terribly wrong.

Lauren drew Carli's left hand closer to her face, seeming to squint to improve her focus in order to assess the small stone.

"Well, my heavens, that's. . .some ring! " she said in an almost chirpy tone, then let Carli's hand drop. It was quickly clasped by another.

"Yes, isn't it, though?" the sleek woman, whom Carli had pegged as being none other than Martha—Mitzi—Dennis coyly agreed.

Carli felt her forced smile falter.

She knew what the catty women meant, and she hoped that Gus didn't, even as she knew that he couldn't help but have interpreted the drift of their meaning.

Suddenly that long-ago Sunday afternoon, and their excitement, shared by Youth Fellowship members and their church family, seemed far, far away, and embarrassingly small-town and provincial when compared to these people's Blue Blood Society Register standards.

As soon as Carli's hands were free she balled them up and shoved them into the pockets of her inexpensive cloth coat. Hers were clearly the hands of a working woman, with her short, carefully trimmed typist's nails maintained to work swiftly and accurately at the keyboard of her computer at the insurance company, while the women present had long, carefully maintained artificial nails that required costly weekly treatments to keep them perfect enough to have been photographed for nail polish advertisements in a slick fashion magazine.

The scent of various perfumes, which no doubt cost hundreds of dollars per ounce, made Carli feel almost lightheaded from the swirling blend, the closeness of the crowd that pressed in on her. She desperately wished that the terminal building floor would somehow miraculously open up and swallow her so she could escape the crush of people forever.

She knew that they were laughing at her—and at Gus—in their mass-produced, off-the-rack clothing and cheap accessories. Mitzi's leather purse had probably cost more than Carli and Gus had spent for a month's rent on their apartment in Virginia! Her heart broke when she realized Gus's ordeal.

Stripped of their jewelry, the men and women gathered there, even the paparazzi who where there on business, but had to dress suitably to be around the rich and the righteous, could have supplied a hefty inventory to start a jewelry store.

Lauren Beekman had said, "That's some ring" in the same manner as a person, upon pulling back a newborn's blanket, and confronting a baby that was precious, but incredibly homely nonetheless, might've offered the waiting parents a dazzling grin and said, "You've got yourself some baby!"

Carli had seen different times how Gus had emotionally detached from an ongoing situation, until it was as if he was not even present when confronted with something that he found unpleasant or painful. She'd never really understood it, nor the ability to do so. But at that instant Carli knew what it was like, for in her mind, she mentally fled the crowded terminal and the shrill persons around her, talking with accents that she found as unusual as she was surer her faint Kentucky twang was to them. She focused on anything to keep from letting the events of the moment fully penetrate her conscious! She prayed that it would soon end, even as a horrible, fearful part of her sensed that this was just the beginning!

Jasper Winthrop came to the rescue, and took Carli into his protective custody. He seemed to sense Carli's misery and the way she was being all but ignored, except to be the focus of a private joke.

"Come with me, dear," he said gently. "I drove to the airport solo, but I'd love to have you and Gus accompany me on the drive to the hospital."

Carli, who felt on the verge of tears, didn't dare speak, but when her eyes flicked up to his she knew that the gratitude she felt was conveyed.

"Oh, but that won't do!" Mitzi Dennis protested in a tone that revealed that she expected to brook no argument. "Gus, darling, you must ride in the limousine with me! It's been so long since I've seen my boy, surely your little wife can spare you for a little while."

To his credit, at least Gus looked in Carli's direction, but before he could say anything, Mitzi pulled him in the opposite direction, and a dour-faced Jasper piffled his fingers at Gus as if to signal him to run along, that his wife would be in good hands.

It was not lost upon Carli that arm-in-arm Gus, his mother, and Lauren Beekman began strolling toward the exit and the waiting chauffeured limousine. Just as they were about to get out of earshot, Carli heard Lauren, who was grinning up at Gus, sweetly and flirtatiously warn:

"We have a lot of catching up to do! I've missed you terribly! You broke my heart, you know. . ."

As the others dispersed, Carli and Jasper Winthrop were left to their own devices.

"What a circus this has become," he sadly remarked as he unlocked his car and assisted Carli in. "I'd wished for a quiet homecoming, something with decorum and respect for everyone's feelings, but of course, that wouldn't do. I doubt that Mitzi has ever done anything quietly in her life, poor woman. Unless she's in the limelight, even if it's only reflected glory from another's stature, or supposed value, the woman's miserable. You won't believe the kinds of people that Mitzi's chosen to keep company with these days."

"I remember reading about her in tabloids at the supermarket checkout lane a few years ago."

Jasper clucked his teeth and sadly shook his head. "They seemed almost like sterling characters to her present-day chums," he said. "Her intimates these days are New Agers, spiritualists, astrology buffs, tarot card readers. . .the entire depraved lot."

"Jasper. . .no!" Carli softly cried, horrified.

"One might say that she didn't exactly gracefully accept Austin's conviction of sin and conversion to Christianity. She's been seeking to find 'the real truth' ever since so that she can enlighten the aging husband she fears has become terribly old-fashioned in his embracing of the Christian faith."

"How awful for him. Especially when he's so ill."

"Instead of it being a time when they can comfort one another as he faces the Lord calling him Home, there've been some unpleasant fusses, even after he was hospitalized, for she wants to intervene with her silly crystals, shamans, and Lord knows what other forms of idolistic frippery while Austin merely wants to draw comfort from his Bible and the Word of God as he's awake and lucid enough to do so."

"I can see why Gus ran away. . ." Carli glumly remarked.

"I shall admit I'm not surprised. You're a bright and intuitive girl, after all, and the woman chosen by the Lord to help Gus Dennis learn how to cut the apron springs and unreasonable family ties that bind him. . .especially those of intergenerational bondage."

Where had she heard that term before? Carli fleetingly mused. But the source evaded her and then Jasper continued saying Gus had made a decision for Christ, but that it would be tested, and tested again, and that his mother, who believed she loved her son, would be doing all in her power to destroy what she considered a simplistic, restricting faith that he might be "freed" by the concepts of New Age religion which she found very much to her liking. It was in reality a new philosophy of faith, Jasper said, that was actually as old as the Father of Lies, the Author of Confusion, the Deceiver. Instead of the philosophies revealing the Lord in Truth, that believers might come to know Him intimately and well, the tenets to which Mitzi and her avant-garde crowd clung allowed them to create God in whatever image they chose, considering themselves as individual gods, en route to perfection and oneness with the universe.

"The Lord has chosen you for a special mission, Carli. I believe that with all of my heart, and I have since the first moment we met. You'll have a fight on your hands to save Gus from the lies and manipulations of his errant, if well-meaning, mother. In the process, I suspect you'll save many more from her depraved and depressing New Age claptrap. Perhaps even Mitzi herself."

"I'm not so sure about that," Carli said, and was helpless not to wipe at a tear that strayed to her eye, quickly followed by another. "She's formidable!"

"I know. . ." Jasper comfortingly acknowledged. "And she's not alone in her unholy crusade, for she's thoroughly convinced poor Lauren of the rightness of her woefully wrong ideas. The poor girl has become Mitzi's favorite proselyte. But remember, my dear girl, and young sister in Christ, 'Greater is He within you. . .' If the Lord is with you, it matters not who is against you, for the Lord will triumph."

"I know," Carli said. And in her head, she did carry that knowledge, but at the moment her heart was sore and fearful with all that had taken place within the last hour.

Helplessly she began to cry.

"It's awful!" she admitted in a squeaky voice. "I feel like I've walked into a movie—late—and everyone knows what's going on but me!"

"There, there. . ." Jasper comforted, then seemed at a loss for anything further to say.

Silence hung heavy for a long moment.

"The next few days will no doubt be among the most difficult," Jasper acknowledged what had already been Carli's realization, "for there's a lot of hullabaloo, both public and private, regarding Gus's return to the family and the corporation. There'll be so much going on in the public realm that you two will have little time in private. I suggest that you use that time to pray for the strength and guidance you'll need to face the personal confrontations ahead."

Carli wiped her nose on a tissue that had already held more tears than it could absorb.

"I expected to see you at the airport, Jasper, and some family members. But not the paparazzi! And I knew you'd said that Austin had become a Christian in the recent past. I had no idea about Gus's mother. . ."

"Unfortunate turn of events, that," he sighed. "More of Mitzi's doings. Emotions in public, she knows how to deal with and handle with aplomb, as if she's an actress, putting on a believable performance. Feelings in private. . .she panics."

"She's an. . .unusual woman," Carli observed, choosing her words carefully, "isn't she? And, gorgeous. I can see why people listen to her. She's a powerful personality. . ."

"That's true, but her power is nothing compared to the strength of Christ," Jasper smiled benevolently. "As for her striking looks—she's had a bit of help along the way," he admitted, referring to various cosmetic surgeries in a benign manner. "But she was Austin's child bride, for he was some fifteen years her senior when they were wed. And hardly natural motherhood material when Gussie was born. Austin spoiled Mitzi too much, I'm afraid, and paid too little attention to Gus. Mitzi is a sad, seeking woman. . .one who is determinedly looking for peace, happiness, and love in all of the wrong places."

"I see," Carli said, hoping he would continue on with his explanations as they drove toward the hospital where her father-in-law was being treated.

As Jasper drove and spoke, occasionally gesturing at landmarks he felt she should notice, she did understand the situation more and more. Even though it didn't make the hurt she felt any less.

Obviously trusting her, Jasper explained that Austin and Mitzi Dennis hadn't a marriage made in heaven, but it was socially convenient, if not quite conventional.

The Dennises stuck it out for the good of their family names, for Mitzi was an heiress in her own right, and for the fact that a messy parting of ways would have cost great sums of money that could be more enjoyably spent or invested elsewhere.

Gus had grown up a lonely, but very bright little boy, who soon learned that life was at its best when he could please and win approval from his high-strung mother, who had little time for him except when she attended his public recitals and performances where it was Gus's goal to excel at whatever he did to make his pretty mother proud.

His father, Austin, who unfortunately had seemed more married to the business than he was interested in a close and fulfilling relationship with his much younger wife, was away so much on business, or working late at the office, to the point where sometimes many days could go by and the little boy wouldn't even see his father. As an older man, who'd been an only child himself, raised similarly to how Gus was being reared, he was not particularly in tune with a young child's need for companionship, a father figure, and whole-hearted approval of his father.

"I was elated to meet you, Carli, and discover that it seemed when it came to choosing a life's companion, Gus Dennis 'broke the mold,' so to speak, and selected a wife not on social merit and connections, but for enduring values of shared faith."

"That's what I thought," Carli said. "Now I'm not so sure."

"Lauren's presence at the media homecoming bother you, my dear?" he asked kindly.

". . .A little bit."

"She and Gus were raised together. . .and are a lot alike. Gus, until he ran off and joined the Navy, was probably the most reliable fellow in her life. She and your mother-in-law are quite close, and I've often thought that it's because they understand one another so well. Poor little rich girls, both of them. Lauren's mother's never been there for her, so Mitzi's filled the void. It's made her feel needed and allows her to bask in the glory of Lauren's looks and accomplishments, for everyone views the girl as Mitzi's protégé."

"Were Gus and Lauren ever. . .?"

"Not the way you are wondering, Carli," Jasper said, shaking his head. "As youngsters they attended the same dance classes, went to the same music teachers, were trundled off to summer camp together. I think everyone assumed that one day they might marry, out of convenience, familiarity, and shared social standing if not true love. But Gus was always more like a big brother to Lauren. Though she's such a flirt, as she, like her mentor, Mitzi Dennis, both seek attention through brusque actions. I'm sure that she's caused many, many people to. . .speculate."

Jasper had told her a lot, and for that she was grateful, but what she really needed was wise counsel on how to proceed, perhaps on the very art of surviving in an environment that was so vastly different and far removed from anything she'd ever known.

"Just be yourself, my dear," he said. "Despite all that I've said, there are people here who'll respond to that and appreciate you for who you are." He slowed and flipped on a turn signal as he entered a lane to enter a large, hospital parking lot. "I know that Austin, for one, will be very well pleased to make your acquaintance. In him, Carli, you'll have a friend."

"I have a feeling I'm going to need a friend."

Jasper gave her a crinkly smile and reached across to pat her hand. "You already have one, Carli. Me!"

"Somehow I've known that since the first moment we've met."

"It says in Scripture to be wise as a serpent, but gentle as a dove, Carli. Let that guide you as you test situations and decide where to invest your trust. In the social strata where the Dennises circulate. . .too many people don't make friends. . . instead, they take hostages."

"I'll remember that. And thank you," Carli said, "for the warning."

"Ready to go in and brave the public?" Jasper asked gently,

"as the wife to the heir of the Dennis millions? And the Dennis Family Defender of the Faith?"

Carli gave a nod that was helplessly bleak. "I guess so. . ."

"Chin up, girl! You're as good as any of them—and better than most!"

"That, too, I shall try to remember," Carli said, managing a weak laugh.

"Then shall we?" Jasper inquired, gallantly offering his arm to Carli.

Together they strode out, and because they were a distance from the hospital entrance, Carli began to sing softly, almost under her breath the opening lyrics to "Onward Christian Soldiers."

Jasper gave a rich, rotund chuckle of agreement, then he cocked his head and looked at her. "My heavens—another surprise. You've a magnificent voice, Caroline Dennis! A true gift from God."

Carli shrugged. "Adequate for someone with little training, I suppose. It's one of the things Gus and I had in common."

And suddenly, as the plate-glass doors automatically swished open to allow them entrance into the massive hospital, Carli idly wondered why she was already talking about her relationship with Gus as if it were in. . .past tense.

More than she liked to admit, she felt like a young woman without the future that had so recently seemed destined to be hers. These feelings persisted even as Jasper Winthrop began to offer comfort that perhaps this sudden and unexpected move to a new region and totally different social realm was an opportunity the Lord had chosen for her that He might use her in a deeper way to bring faith to a faithless society and minister to mankind in a larger, and more far-reaching way.

eight

Entering the hospital complex was almost like journeying into a world within the real world, where outside realities seemed suspended in order to deal with the unbending, clock-dominated, day-in-day-out routine of caring for the ill.

The massive brick, steel, and glass structure, surrounded by parking garages, was self-contained, as if it created a little village within the major city surrounding the vast building complex.

There was a cafeteria, gift shop, florist nook, shoeshine station, and other services to make the lives of those relegated to the healing routines conducted around-the-clock a little easier as they made the transition.

No one paid much attention to Carli Dennis and Jasper Winthrop as they passed through the comfortable, if impersonal, lobby, their heels clacking on the marble floors as they made their way toward the bank of elevators.

It took a moment for an available elevator to stop to convey them. Jasper tapped the appropriate button, but the mechanism ground to a halt at each successive floor to let people out or take on riders.

The beige, immaculately clean cubicle was jammed with visitors and uniform-clad hospital personnel before the doors hushed open to disgorge passengers in front of the color-coordinated nurses' station that guarded the vestibule leading to the private wing. It was in this wing that Austin Dennis, Jr., was cared for in a self-contained, very private Intensive Care Unit reserved for those who could afford the round-the-clock private duty nursing care.

The charge nurse, bent over the shoulder of one of the ward nurses who was entering data at a computer terminal, flicked her gaze up to scrutinize those who were alighting on the floor she clearly viewed as her domain.

Her eyes flashed a studied wariness when she caught sight of Jasper Winthrop, but an instant later she dropped her guard and relaxed, smiling at the elderly gentleman who accompanied Carli.

"Hello, Mr. Winthrop!" she greeted. "We've missed seeing you lately."

"I was out of town on business," he admitted.

"Glad that you're okay. People at services on Sunday morning were wondering. . . Your trip was successful?"

"Things couldn't have gone better, Nurse Hathaway," he said, grinning, and then patted Carli's arm. "I located Austin's son. This is his wife, Caroline, known as Carli to her friends. She's a fine Christian girl; I've enjoyed getting to know her."

"How wonderful!"

Jasper Winthrop made introductions, and Carli and Nurse Sharon Hathaway seemed to feel mutually at ease with one another, especially when Carli realized that Jasper and Nurse Hathaway had met at church and seemed to belong to a friendly, family-oriented congregation like that which she and Gus had just left behind.

"How's Austin today?" Jasper inquired.

"About the same," Nurse Hathaway said in a careful tone, which Carli well remembered from her father's long hospitalization toward the end of his life.

"Is he up to a bit of company?"

"Oh. . .I think so!" Nurse Hathaway said brightly. "Especially company that he's been so looking forward to arriving. Your visits always seem to brighten his days and rejuvenate him, Jasper. And we both know that he's been pining for his son, waiting for him to return. . ."

"This will be a special day for Austin," the nurse said as she led the way down the quiet, well-maintained, pristine corridor in a well-staffed wing that clearly housed state-of-the-art equipment.

"Gus should be along any moment. He rode with his mother; she insisted," Jasper explained.

With the mention of the senior Mrs. Dennis, Carli believed

that she saw a faint hint of tension creep into the charge nurse's stance. She sensed that the professional caregiver was less than elated to know she was about to face Mitzi Dennis.

"Sharon—Nurse Hathaway—and Mitzi have crossed swords a few times since Austin was hospitalized," Jasper confided.

Sharon Hathaway, BSN, paused in the corridor. "It's begun to feel like 'countless' times rather than just 'a few'," she clarified.

"Mrs. Dennis and her New Ager cohorts have led poor Nurse Hathaway on quite a merry chase some days."

"Merry, Jasper?" the nurse chided. "I think not. Ridiculous—yes! Amusing—no!"

Jasper gave the long-suffering nurse an encouraging pat on her shoulder that was comfortably encased in mauve scrubs. "Mitzi and her fellow believers and parapsychology gurus and metaphysical chums have created quite the commotion in the past few months."

"An understatement, my friend," Sharon Hathaway suggested. She faced Carli, who she seemed to have considered an instant friend. "I had to call the administrator at home one evening to put a stop to the strange goings-on."

Jasper offered a weak smile. "As you can imagine, Carli, Mrs. Dennis didn't like that at all. Especially after all of the funding that Dennis Mining and Manufacturing has provided here over the years. She has tried to use that as influence to circumvent the regulations and standard operating procedures."

"We can offer great appreciation to major donors, but she seemed unable to understand that we can't give approval for treatments that are quackery and flimflam, bordering on shamanism and witch doctor cures, especially when it disturbs other patients and prevents the staff from carrying out orders and fulfilling care plans."

Although Carli simply listened, she shuddered inwardly at what had transpired, and sensed that Nurse Hathaway, who seemed professional and fearless when faced with those who claimed rank and privilege, had found Mitzi Dennis as frustrating as had she.

"The other week Mitzi caught a curtain on fire with all the candles she insisted on keeping lit in Austin's room."

"Aromatherapy," Nurse Hathaway explained to Carli in a disdainful tone.

"The week before that it was crystals," Jasper recalled.

"Mrs. Dennis had more colorful stones littering the ICU and bedside than would've been needed to have stocked a large aquarium to overflowing. Each one was neatly imprinted in gold with what aspects of life or emotion they were supposed to improve, and every little rock came with its own satin-lined, velvet, drawstring jeweler's bag."

"No doubt she paid dearly for them."

"Indeed she did!" Nurse Hathaway sniffed. "And I hate to consider what she paid for the. . .white witch she claims called special powers into the stones."

"A. . .witch?!" Carli gasped.

"A witch," Nurse Hathaway affirmed. "And you know, as well as Jasper and I do, that there's no such thing as a white witch, or 'good witch.' A witch is a witch!"

"Oh. . .heavens. . ." Carli whispered as she began to see what she—and Gus—would be dealing with upon the return to the Dennis family fold and his powerful, determined mother's influence.

"Not long ago, she also tried guided imagery and visualizations. She carted a CD player up here and brought along compact discs of some kind of Eastern Indian music and chants. She attempted to convince Mr. Dennis to close his eyes and imagine himself well. . .but every time he closed his eyes. . .he promptly fell asleep and when he started to snore, she shook him awake!"

Carli couldn't help smiling at the picture those words created in her mind.

"She's put you through a lot," she commiserated.

"She's putting herself through the worst treatment in her sad, sick seeking," Jasper pointed out.

"She's opening a lot of forbidden doors, whether she realizes it or not," Nurse Hathaway said. "Scriptures make that perfectly clear!"

"It's not doing anything for Austin's morale, either," Jasper sadly reported. "It worries him terribly. He so wishes that Mitzi would share his faith. And. . .his son. . .Gus does, I'm delighted to report."

"Praise God! What good news!" Nurse Hathaway said. "There's hope for Mrs. Dennis, of course."

"Especially if we, and our congregation, continue to pray for the poor lost people who so ignorantly place their faith in what they consider new and wonderfully revealed faiths."

"When the truth is that the New Age untruths are as old as the Father of Lies himself!" Sharon said.

A moment later the three entered Austin Dennis's sickroom.

Sharon Hathaway plumped his pillow, patted his arm, eyed the various monitors and equipment and encouraged him to enjoy a brief visit with his longtime friend and his new daughter-in-law.

Carli had been nervous about meeting the elderly Mr. Dennis, but she realized it had been concern suffered in vain, for he was a pleasant, grandfather-like man, and even though he was gravely and terminally ill, he did his best to joke and make others in his presence feel at ease.

When he offered a whispery, thin-voiced testimony to the Lord's goodness, and how he looked forward to Glory and being with the Lord and all the saints forever, tears glimmered in Carli's eyes.

A moment later, Sharon returned.

"I hate to suggest you leave," she told Jasper and Carli, "but Mr. Dennis's vitals are signaling that he's getting tired. He should rest up before more visitors arrive."

"Take a nap, old chap," Jasper said. "Carli and I will get a cup of coffee in the cafeteria. Carli, I'll leave you two alone for a moment and wait in the corridor."

"Rest well, Dad," Carli said, and kissed his cheek that had been smoothly shaven by an orderly that morning. "Gus will be here soon. And I know that he's going to be a son in whom you are very well pleased."

"I'm a blessed man to get such a daughter in my older years," Austin Dennis said, clasping Carli's hand, then bringing it to his lips to press a feathery, fervent kiss to the soft skin. "With the grace of God, try to be a daughter to my Mitzi even if she won't be much of a mother to you. I want you to . . .and Gus needs you to."

"I know," Carli said, feeling that the words summed up both knowledge of the situation and a promise given.

"It is right for a man to leave his father and mother and cleave to his wife that the two shall become one," Austin Dennis whispered. "I won't be here long to intervene. Don't let Mitzi put asunder what the Lord God has joined together."

"Where Gus goes, I will follow," Carli promised.

Austin gave a faint shake of his head, which he seemed almost too exhausted to move.

"Only if the Lord God continues to lead him," he whispered.

Then Austin Dennis, Sr., closed his eyes and slid into a light doze. Carli touched his hand with complete and unconditional love that came so naturally when dealing with other committed Christians, then quietly left the room.

"Coffee, my dear?" Jasper inquired.

"Love some. But it's my treat," Carli said.

"If you insist," Jasper said, slipping his arm to loop through hers. "Next time I'm buying."

"It's a deal," Carli agreed. "I'd like to spend as much time with Dad Dennis as we're able."

" 'Tis my hope that Gus will share your sentiments."

Carli looked at him, a bit alarmed. "What do you mean by that?"

"They should've been here by now," he said. "Even if there was a traffic tie-up due to an accident, they're long overdue. Knowing Mitzi, she probably detoured Gus so that they went by corporate headquarters, and probably the Dennis mansion prior to that, before attending to the most pressing business—that of reuniting a gravely ill, grieving man with the son he loves and longs to see again."

A half an hour later, a tired Carli and a silent, reflective Jasper Winthrop rode the elevator up to the floor that housed the private hospital suites.

To allow Mr. Dennis to rest up, they waited in a cozy

solarium not far removed from the nurses' station. As weary as Carli was she leaned her head back, closed her eyes, and was almost asleep while Mr. Winthrop read a magazine, when there was a commotion as the elevator doors opened.

Carli flipped her eyes open, so tired that momentarily she felt disoriented as she was caught between sleep and complete wakefulness. For a moment she stared at the small group of people, greatly reduced compared to the throng at the airport, but accompanied by one lone professional photographer weighted down with his costly equipment.

Nurse Hathaway stood before the group, an invisible mantle of authority drawn about her.

"Only one visitor at a time," she ordered. "And immediate family members only!"

She gave Lauren Beekman and the bearded, shaggy-haired, heavyset photographer an unflinching gaze. Sighing, Lauren turned away to wait in the solarium. The photographer merely adjusted the webbing of his equipment and looked to Mitzi Dennis.

"But we promised Mr. McCarthy an exclusive," Mitzi protested.

"You shouldn't make promises that are not within your authority to keep, Mrs. Dennis," Nurse Hathaway said calmly.

"We'll see about this!" Mitzi hissed, glaring.

Carli's heart was in her throat. She scarcely recognized her husband! Gus was dressed in what had to have been at least a five-hundred-dollar suit left over from his days within his parent's home, and shoes that were so costly the price could've fed a family for several weeks. On his wrist. . .was a Rolex watch.

But it was the expression on his face that bothered Carli, not the wardrobe in which he had appeared. For Gus Dennis seemed reduced in stature, although he stood almost six feet tall, to being a lonely little boy who desperately wished to please his mother.

"One at a time," Nurse Hathaway repeated. "Gus?" She said and shook his hand. "Let's start with you."

A part of Carli wanted to be there for Gus, but she knew

that the reunion was something he had to do by himself, that it was appropriate that he be alone with his father. Carli prayed that it would go well, and she found herself praying that she could remove Gus from Dennis Mining and Manufacturing, that they could return to the life that had so recently been theirs, an existence that was comfortable, casual, close, with easy communication.

But deep down, she sensed that it was not to be.

Already people were speaking to Gus in tones that were deferential. It was as if somehow the authority had already been passed from dying father to youthful son, merely by the mere fact of his presence.

"Up to being the wife of a CEO?" Gus's question returned to haunt her.

She considered it anew.

If to be the wife of a CEO she had to become like Mitzi Dennis, she vowed that she would leave forever before she would stay and be transformed into a woman who would find it difficult to look into a mirror and meet her own condemning eyes.

nine

As Carli waited at the hospital until the visit was deemed concluded and the hospital routine must be served, she sensed that despite the stressful difficulties of the day she'd had so far, that the misery would escalate when they left for the Dennis compound. At that point, Jasper Winthrop, who'd been her constant companion and social protector, would return to his own residence while she'd be transported to the Dennis mansion, knowing that she would feel like a foreigner in a strange and hostile land.

It helped immensely when Gus took her hand in his as they headed for the elevator and the waiting limousine.

"Ready to go, darling?" he inquired.

Carli gratefully smiled up at him, but didn't speak, settling for a simple nod. It hadn't been lost on her that every time she'd opened her mouth, Mitzi Dennis had winced as if she'd heard nails raking across a blackboard upon hearing Carli's Kentucky accent that Gus had claimed to find so charming and musical when they'd first met.

Little was said on the drive away from the hospital. Gus seemed distant and detached, preoccupied with all that had taken place and everything that lay before them. Carli focused on the landmarks that they passed as the uniformed driver jockeyed the large white limousine through the traffic-choked streets.

Carli felt her nerves tightening with growing apprehension as the driver guided the car onto streets that led to more secluded areas of the city where the vast estates lining both sides of the street quietly bespoke wealth, power, and privilege to any who chanced to pass by.

"It's not far now," Gus broke the silence to announce as the driver slowed, turned a corner, then negotiated a hill that led to a brick and iron enclosure. The sturdy wall, which no doubt dated to the turn of the century, was twined with a thick covering of ivy vines that had obviously crawled along and clung to the masonry for decades, all but blocking the huge, sprawling mansion from the public's view.

Towering hardwood trees, which had weathered the seasons for a century or more each, seemed to stand sentry around the castlelike Bedford stone structure. Thick and massive evergreens were almost like servile growths nestled around the hardwoods' trunks.

The limousine driver activated his turn signal, then reached for an unobtrusive button on the dash, pressed it, and the majestic, ornately decorated locked front gates seemed to yawn open to allow them entrance.

The long driveway hadn't a pebble out of place. Shrubbery, which had been trimmed with excruciating exactness, flanked the private roadway. English garden-style areas, carefully designed, constructed, and maintained, dotted the sweeping, immaculate groomed lawn that contained statuary so elegant and complementary to the landscape that the huge marble masterpieces looked as if they'd gently pushed their way up through the tender, rich earth to almost come to life in a stance of perfect permanence.

The mansion was as aesthetically appealing from the outside as a scale model collector's dollhouse from Nieman-Marcus. The windows and draperies were as appealing from the exterior as they were beautiful items of decor to perfectly complement the professionally designed rooms of the residence.

"Home, sweet home. . .again! " Gus said, sighing with content, referring to the earlier quick-change stop that Mitzi had worked into their busy afternoon schedule after departing Logan International Airport.

For a moment Carli felt stung, then sad, when she recalled the many times Gus had come home from the pizzeria, the scent of pepperoni clinging to his clothes, and murmured, "Home, sweet home," flopping into the worn but incredibly comfortable recliner in their small apartment.

How ratty and awful their first home must seem to him by

comparison! Was he now wondering how he could've ever thought he had been happy in such a dwelling that now had to seem embarrassingly shabby to him?

The driver assisted them from the vehicle, and the family butler, Staunton, met them at the front door. He relieved them of their wraps and offered willingness to fetch refreshments or set into action whatever plans they desired to make their homecoming more pleasant.

For Gus, the transition seemed easy, almost as if he'd never been away, Carli suspected, so glad was everyone to see him, and so at home he obviously felt.

For Carli it was wretchedly difficult.

The Dennis mansion wasn't home in her view, and she knew that it would be like residing in a museum where so many objects were to be viewed but not touched or used.

Servants were everywhere, it seemed. Silent, respectful, unobtrusive, but nevertheless there, and Carli felt unnerved, knowing that she would find it disconcerting to realize that her every movement could be monitored and reported back to others.

"Staunton, would you show Caroline to the suite she'll be occupying, please? Gus and I have business to discuss," Mitzi crisply explained. "And, of course, Gus needs no introduction to the quarters."

"This way, please," Staunton invited, giving Carli a faint bow and a noncommittal smile before he led her from the large, denlike library. Carefully he turned back, pausing to securely close the double doors behind them.

"I trust you'll be very comfortable here, Miss Caroline," Staunton assured as he led her toward the plush carpeted curved wooden stairway that led to the second floor. Rooms on the second floor all faced out over the downstairs area below which reminded Carli of an elaborate, lush, but impersonal lobby of a five-star hotel.

"These are your quarters," Staunton announced, opening a heavy, solid wood door. "I'm sure you'll find the suite to your liking."

There was a large bath, quaint and cozy sitting room, large

luxuriously appointed bedroom, and a tremendous amount of concealed storage space. Exquisite silk flower arrangements and expensive oil paintings created investment-quality focal pieces to accent the artfully selected decor.

"It's beautiful," Carli murmured.

Obediently Carli followed at Staunton's heels as he revealed the storage space arrangements to her. If anything was not to her liking, he affirmed, she was to let him know immediately and he would attend to the matter at once and the staff would be prompt and attentive in providing her desires.

"Thank you for showing me around," Carli said, hoping that she'd be left alone at last so that she could think and try to comprehend all that had so drastically changed in her life.

"My pleasure, indeed," Staunton said, and gave another neat little bow. "If you need anything just ring," he said and gestured to the electronic system. "Now, if you'll excuse me, Miss Caroline, I'm off to oversee the preparations for the evening meal. We'll dine at six o'clock straight-up. And. . . it's formal."

With that announcement Carli looked down at her simple dove-gray dress, matching hair ornament used to hold her long, curly hair away from her face, and her coordinating accessories. Staunton seemed to sense her uncertainty. He gave Carli what she recognized as a genuine smile, not a practiced expression.

"Your attire is perfectly in order, Miss Caroline."

"Thank you," she replied, grateful for his reassurance.

"The dinnerware," Staunton said softly. "Always remember—use your silverware from the outside in."

"Got it!" Carli whispered. "Thanks again," she repeated, feeling that at least within the household there lay a potential ally.

"I trust you'll wish to unpack?"

"Yes," Carli said.

"And you can find your own way to return to Gus and his mother when they've concluded their meeting."

"No problem," Carli assured and with a quick smile dismissed Staunton to go about his routine business while she faced what seemed like the gargantuan task of making adjustments and dealing with what she recognized as a form of cultural shock.

Fifteen minutes later Carli softly closed the upstairs door behind her, quietly made her way down the staircase, crossed the dimly lit central room, then proceeded down the short, heavily carpeted hallway that led to the cloistered library area. Potted palms and matching statues on either side of the door seemed to stand guard over the private area.

Carli was about to rap on one of the huge, eight-foot double doors that let into the high-ceilinged, book-lined room, when Mitzi Dennis's curdling, scornful laughter caused her to freeze in mid-action, her heart thudding.

"Oh Gus, you pitiful fool! How could you have been so shortsighted and stupid?" Mitzi Dennis inquired in a scolding, scathing tone that was just audible where Carli stood, frozen, outside the closed library doors.

Whatever Gus's response, it was a low-toned, indecipherable mumble.

"How could you have settled for marrying a poor, meek little church mouse when you could have had your pick of sleek and wealthy women with the social sheen of sables? You chose a valueless, common, industrious little brown wren for a pet and plaything when you could have so easily had someone unusual and a social flamingo!"

"Your analogy is for the birds, Mother! You're not being fair to Carli. . .Caroline!"

"What you did to the Dennis dynasty isn't fair, Gus! Not after all of the Dennis men who've given their lives to build what you inherit with such ease and prestige. If you want the Dennis empire to last, get rid of your sweet, naive little hillbilly, Gus, while you still can, and do it inexpensively."

"No! I love Carli. . .Caroline. . ."

"You're just being stubborn and defiant. If I say something's black, you say it's white. You've always been that way, ever since you were a little boy! If you want to please me, Gus, get rid of her. And if what your father's bequeathed to you means anything, for his sake, do the right thing! Make his dying days happy!"

"Dad likes. . .Caroline," Gus protested.

"He's under so much sedation sometimes he scarcely knows his own name. Go ahead. Break your father's heart. And mine," Mitzi said. "But mark my word, someday you'll know that I—we—were right."

"Never!"

There was a strained silence. Carli considered knocking, but then realized she'd be at a loss for what to say, to either of them. She'd known that Gus's mother had taken an instant dislike to her, very probably made up her mind long before they ever met face-to-face, but Carli was not feeling strong enough to deal with an outright confrontation. Nor was she quite willing to trust that Gus would wholeheartedly take her side, for she'd already seen so many strange and alarming changes since he'd returned to his family and the ways of his raising.

The silence was broken by Mitzi's voice that was as low and lethal as a cocked pistol.

"If you're not intelligent enough, nor man enough to end it, then I will!"

"Don't you dare!" Gus flared. "Why can't you mind your own business, Mother?"

"You tend to Dennis Mining and Manufacturing business, my dear boy, and I will mind what I feel is my business."

"Leave Carli alone. Don't do something stupid, Mother. I'm warning you."

Her chuckle was chiding. "Do you take me for an artless fool?"

"Dad's always let you have your way, Mother, and you've run over people roughshod. But at his request, and as soon as the papers are signed, he'll no longer be in charge, Mother, and I will be taking up the reins. You'll be properly and comfortably cared for. But I can arrange to have you put on a very short leash."

Mitzi laughed as if the idea were preposterous, a petulant child's powerless threat.

"All I plan on doing, Gus, is playing out enough rope with

which to allow your darling little Caroline to hang herself. Given time, she'll manage that, and quite handily, I'm sure. Since you seem so grimly determined to defy me and the society to which we belong, please, at least have enough social finesse to do something about reinventing your little wife into someone more socially acceptable."

"I plan to," Gus informed in an even, businesslike, somewhat chilly tone. "You'll see."

"Ah, but it'll take more than a new wardrobe and the work of an excellent hairstylist to turn her into. . .our kind of person."

"A normal mother-in-law might enjoy helping a daughter-in-law to adjust."

Mitzi's voice was mocking. "No one's ever accused me of being average. Anyway, I'm sure that neither of us would enjoy such a collaboration. We haven't so much as one thing in common."

"That's where you're wrong. You have me in common."

Mitzi sniffed concession. "Surely that's all."

"As a matter of fact, it's not."

"No? What else could we possibly share?"

"Your rare blood type. You're both universal donors."

"That's a grand start. For my part, I'd rather than die than accept her blood—and—"

Even Mitzi Dennis wasn't heartless enough to give voice to the emotion that she'd watch Carli Dennis pass away before she'd share her life's blood that her son's wife might live.

"Someone will have to help Car—Caroline—make the adjustments," Gus sighed.

"I have far too many social obligations as it is. But, I'm sure that Lauren Beekman would lend you a hand. In the past, as you may recall, anytime you called, Lauren came running. I'm sure things haven't changed, Gus. And Lauren always has liked a challenge. This entire debacle might be just her cup of tea."

"I don't know about that. . ." Gus replied, his tone weak. "There's always Jasper. Or even Staunton."

"Or Cinderella's fairy godmother if you can find her."

"When it comes to fairies and witches and wizards and magicians, I'm sure that your address book is ripe with contacts."

"At least they're honest, interesting, and intriguingly avant-garde and open-minded, which is much more than I know we can expect from your little Southern belle Bible-thumper!"

"As far as I'm concerned, Mother, this meeting is finished!"

Carli, who'd been frozen into inaction, came to life with the desperation and speed required of pure survival. She fled to the upstairs quarters, praying that Gus wouldn't follow her, hoping, even so, that he would, and that he'd hold her tightly, kiss away the tears, reassure her that everything was going to be all right and that they wouldn't have to remain in Boston much longer.

But Carli knew that such thoughts were folly. She had seen the handwriting on the wall, so to speak, and she knew that already there were documents in black and white, waiting to be signed, which would mean that there was no going back, only forward. And with the help of God, and His intervention and guidance, she prayed that she would face it all, survive, and triumph over adversity.

ten

It was almost dawn before Gus finally came to their assigned quarters, showered, and prepared for bed. Carli had quietly cried for what seemed hours after she'd fled upstairs after overhearing part of Gus's and his mother's heated discussion regarding her.

Staunton had come upstairs to rap on her door to summon her to dinner. Carli had carefully modulated her voice to hide the fact that she had been crying, and she begged off, using being overtired as an excuse to avoid dining with Gus and his mother. Staunton had left it at that after making sure that she was aware that if she later found herself hungry she could ring the kitchen and the staff would prepare a tray to be brought up to her room.

Carli felt numb as she showered, shampooed and prepared for bed. She found herself simultaneously both hoping that Gus would join her, so they could talk and get everything out in the open, and that he wouldn't arrive upstairs to witness her in such a state of devastation.

Carli's eyes felt gritty from tears by the time she drifted off to sleep, periodically jolting awake, as if in a nightmare, except that the churning subconscious fears were her actual reality now.

"Where've you been. . .?" Carli asked in a sleepy tone when Gus snapped out the bedside lamp.

"Reading," he explained, yawning.

"Must've been a real page-turner," Carli offered lightly, doing her best to foster casual conversation.

"Hardly," Gus wearily corrected. "I've been in the den at the desk Dad used as his in-home office space, sifting through stacks and stacks of company statements, quarterly reports to stockholders, prospectus materials. . .and gearing up trying to get up-to-speed in time for the ten o'clock meeting with department heads and the corporate staff. And a press conference following that. . ."

"Oh. Hardly escapist reading."

"Faced with columns of percentage points, numerical facts, and various cumulative earning statistics, I found myself escaping, all right, into nodding off to sleep. I figured I might as well pack it in and get some sleep. There's no way I can cram in any more data for absorption right now."

Carli took Gus's hand, and he gave hers an appreciative and encouraging squeeze. "It's been a long day, and a tough one, for both of us."

"Today will be every bit as long. I told Staunton not to let me sleep past eight-thirty. I need time to organize my thoughts and jot down a few notes to get me through the press conference, which will definitely make news in the *Boston Globe* and no doubt warrant a mention in *The Wall Street Journal*."

"Poor Gus," Carli murmured. She stroked his brow, then pressed a kiss to his cheek. He snugged his arm around her and she leaned her head on his shoulder, brushing a wing of dark hair away from her face.

"Gus?"

"Ummmm?"

"You really looked nice in a business suit today. I was impressed."

"Clothes do make the man sometimes," he pointed out. "Kind of a change from the pizzeria uniform and baseball cap," he said, giving a soft, self-deprecating laugh.

". . .I guess those days are behind us."

"I guess so. Now you're the wife of a CEO of a Fortune 500 company instead of an office worker at an insurance corporation."

Carli took a deep breath. "I suppose I'll need some new clothes, too, won't I?"

Gus patted her. "Don't worry, sweet. We can afford 'em."

"I know. I just don't know where to go.Or what to buy."

"You'll no doubt suffer sticker-shock when you flip over the price tags, hon. But don't worry about it. Simply sign your name on the store receipts. They know where to send the bills. Mother does business with the stores all the time."

"I don't even know where to start. . ." Carli admitted, trying to keep her voice from conveying she felt bleak and overwhelmed by the prospect.

Gus named a half a dozen exclusive shops. "Any, or all, of them will do."

Carli noticed that Gus had seemed relieved to have the topic of a new wardrobe for her raised for discussion, and that he'd believed the idea to be hers, never suspecting that she'd overheard his mother's caustic remarks.

"I'll take care of it right away," Carli said. "I'm sure the shop clerks can assist me. I can call a taxi to take me to the stores if you write down the names and I can look up business locations in the telephone directory."

"That won't be necessary," Gus said. "We have a limousine service we use and pay the tab once a month."

"Oh."

"Mother keeps our driver quite busy all by herself."

"Okay. I'll manage it. Somehow. . ."

"I can arrange for someone to go with you," Gus offered.

Carli's heart sank. *Who? Lauren Beekmen, Mitzi Dennis's protégé? Donkeys would fly before I agree to that,* she thought, her inner emotions steely and determined.

"I'm a big girl," Carli said in a light tone. "I'll manage."

"Perhaps Uncle Jasper could go with you," Gus suggested. "He's quite the old gent as you've already discovered."

"Oh. . .great idea!" Carli gushed, relief flowing through her.

"Uncle Jasper told me yesterday afternoon that he'd call in the morning to see if I wanted a ride to the hospital or anything."

"Then I guess it's settled," Gus said, yawning.

"It seems that it is," Carli said, feeling a lot better and much more secure about everything, and about Gus, who now seemed as close to her, as kind, as thoughtful, patient and understanding as he'd appeared emotionally distant, detached, even callous the afternoon before when it seemed that he had donned not only expensive, top-of-the-line tailored clothing and shoes, but wore an aura of the business executive on the rise, and that nothing—and no one—would stand in the way of his confidently taking over the helm.

"Carli?" Gus spoke, as if testing to see if she was still awake. His whisper was soft, strained, faint in the darkness.

"Uh–huh?"

"When you're out buying clothes be sure to get something suitable to wear to a funeral." Gus paused, choked by emotion that Carli realized he struggled to suppress. "Dad's not going to be with us. . .much longer."

"Oh, Gus. . .I know."

"He was waiting for me to come home. He told me so. He's at peace. He's ready to die. Looking forward to being with the Lord."

"I know."

"I wasn't the son I could've been, Carli."

"You're only human. You are now, Gus. That's what matters. And as a Christian son you're a son in whom he's very well pleased."

"But those years are lost to us forever."

"That was probably what was needed for the Lord to find you willing to be drawn to Him as your Heavenly Father. To teach you to rely on Him, not the Dennis dynasty."

"If only I'd been here. . ."

Then we wouldn't have even met, Carli started to say but veered away from stating what she realized had been Mitzi Dennis's main concern.

"You'll have eternity together, loving one another and all the believers, worshipping God together for all time."

"Thanks for reminding me of that," Gus said.

He was quiet a long moment, reflective, and Carli was, too, as she considered what lay ahead of them in the coming days. "I've got to stop arguing so much with Mother, too," Gus finally broke the stillness. "This isn't easy for her."

"I know," Carli agreed, and refrained from voicing the view that Mitzi Dennis brought a lot of difficulties upon herself and those around her with her manipulative manner and ruthless behavior.

"I haven't been the kind of son to Mother that I could've been."

She hasn't been a real mother to you! The protesting thought seared Carli's mind. "She needs our prayers," Carli said instead.

"I've got to stop fighting with her. She enjoys it entirely too much. It's like she's addicted to criticism, arguing, and trying to reshape the world and everyone in it into her idea of utopia with everyone doing exactly as she would prefer."

Carli couldn't have agreed more, but didn't admit that to her husband.

"I don't know how to handle her. She's so mercurial, and volatile as TNT!"

"'A kind word turns away wrath,' " Carli reminded.

Gus gave Carli a quick hug. "You're so right."

"The Lord's ways are never wrong."

"I need to behave more agreeably toward Mother, and not let her goad me into using her own nasty techniques and treating her as she does others. I suppose I need to offer concessions, even swallow my anger and placate her. These are difficult times for her, too, and she needs support and unconditional love and acceptance, not defiance, derision. . ."

Carli said nothing, but her mind seemed to sear with the feelings that Gus couldn't—and shouldn't—compromise simply to keep peace with his mother, especially when she was in gross error and her behaviors were at odds with the ways of the Lord and God's people.

She sensed what she should say, *Love the sinner while hating the sin,* but it was as if the words were stuck in her throat, and as if the previous day's events had so shattered her basic trust level in Gus that she wasn't sure that to make such a remark wouldn't cause him to be defensive and argumentative with her in defending his mother. She was afraid that she risked sounding judgmental or self-righteous or even simply mean-spirited in pointing out that his mother was a woman who flaunted her worldly ways and scorned the previously held beliefs of those who trusted in Jesus Christ as their Lord and Savior.

Then Carli realized it was too late to say anything along those lines, anyway, at least at the moment, for an exhausted Gus Dennis had dropped off to sleep.

☙

Carli awakened and dreaded trying to shake Gus awake when he'd had so little sleep, but she knew that they both had to arise and prepare to face another day that promised to be as rigorous, stressful, and emotionally charged.

Mitzi Dennis was nowhere in sight which made Carli's morning easier as she dressed. She shared a quiet breakfast with her husband before his father's car was brought around for him to have at his disposal as he left for the office complex to face meetings, probably a business lunch, and then a visit with his father. He would return to the Dennis mansion late that night to unwind for a little while before he faced another marathon session trying to absorb the directions in which the family business had grown since he'd left the area.

Before leaving, Gus took a moment to give Carli a little parchment card with about a dozen important numbers neatly printed on it.

"Keep this in your purse for easy reference," Gus said. "You'll have to add my cell-phone number to it as soon as I find out what it is and pick up the phone. Add my pager number, too."

"Okay. . ." Carli said, weathering another spurt of realizing how drastically their lives had changed in the past forty-eight hours.

"I'll have someone make arrangements so you have your own cell phone, too, hon. They're important, not just for communication but nowadays, for security."

"I see. . ."

"I'm not sure that you do, Carli," Gus said in a quiet tone. "You'll have to be on guard. You won't be able to be as trusting as you've been in the past. There are people—strangers—who won't hesitate to harm you if they know it would hurt me. Until you know your way around Boston, please see that you're in the company of someone trustworthy."

Carli's heart froze. Was he referring to her being kidnapped? Held for ransom that a criminal could hope that the Dennis family would gladly pay for her safe return? Carli almost laughed out loud at the idea. Wouldn't that be an answer to Mitzi Dennis's prayers to the strange powers and false gods in whom the woman placed her faith?

Carli had concluded that Gus's mother didn't merely have a few rocks in her head, she had them everywhere. Placed around the mansion like beautiful, natural, breathtaking "objects d'art" were geodes and unusual prehistoric stone formations that could be admired for their beauty, but which Mitzi Dennis trusted to keep her, and her loved ones, safe, wealthy, happy, living lives of great blessings because of the auras and magnetic vibrations the immobile crystals were said to emanate.

"I'll be careful," Carli promised.

"See you tonight," Gus said, kissing Carli good-bye. "I'll be home in time for dinner."

"I'll be waiting," Carli said, and felt a sad bereftness that she wouldn't be preparing one of Gus's favorite meals, but instead would be, like he, unaware of what the cook was even serving until the shiny metallic dome was removed from her plate at the table glittering with sterling candelabras and the best china money could buy.

Carli glanced at the card Gus had given her. Jasper Winthrop's number was at the top of the list and Carli was trying to work up the courage to dial his number. She feared that she might awaken him. He'd had an exhausting day, too, after all.

"You've a caller, Miss Caroline," Staunton informed as he approached Carli. "Mr. Winthrop is waiting in the main room to see you."

"Oh. . .great!" Carli said, her relief and joy at the news so great that Staunton's face twitched as he suppressed a grin at her enthusiasm.

"Thank you for summoning me, Staunton," Carli remembered her new high-society manners.

"My pleasure, Miss Caroline," he assured.

Carli rushed to where Uncle Jasper waited. She was so happy to see him that she flung her arms around him and accepted his equally warm hug that did much to relieve the continuous chill caused by residing in Mitzi Dennis's private domain.

"It's so good to see you, Uncle Jasper. You look rested. Sleep well?"

"Wonderfully! I feel great."

"You look it. I hope you can offer me some help today," Carli said, and lowered her tone, sketching in her needs. "Do you think you can spare the time?"

"Of course! I'm retired now, dear girl, so my services are at your disposal. We'll attend to your shopping needs, then have lunch, and drop by the hospital as well."

"Terrific!" Carli cried. "Let me get my coat and purse. I'll be ready in a jiffy!"

Rather than have Carli rush off to hunt for her wrap, Jasper Winthrop raised his voice slightly. "Staunton, my good man, would you be so kind as to fetch the young Mrs. Dennis's wrap, please? We're off to be about the town."

"Right away, sir," Staunton replied, and offered a little bow as he turned away and returned a moment later with all that Carli would need. Gallantly he helped her into her coat.

"Thank you, Staunton," she murmured.

He gave her shoulder a gentle pat as he smoothed the fabric and collar into place.

"My pleasure, Miss Carli," he replied, smiling down at her with kindly, approving eyes.

"Shall we go?" Jasper inquired, offering Carli his arm as Staunton moved to get the door.

Jasper's car was waiting at curbside. After tucking Carli in, he took his place behind the wheel, then gave a rich chuckle as he secured his seat belt.

"Well, I must admit, my dear, I liked the sound of that! "

"Liked what?"

"Didn't you notice? Staunton called you 'Miss Carli'. It seems that you've already won over the Dennis family butler. You've a friend in Staunton, Carli. He's a good man. You can trust him. Of course, he's placed his loyalties where they should be, while offering impeccable service to all who visit at the Dennis mansion, whether he approves of them or not."

"Praise God! I can use all of the friends I can acquire."

"You've another friend, too, Carli, whether you realize it or not."

"Really? Who?"

"Nurse Sharon Hathaway. She likes you very, very much."

"She was nice to me. I thought perhaps it was simply her professional manner. I can tell she's very good at what she does."

"She has a true gift of healing and God-given compassion. And strength. She likes you personally, not just professionally."

"I liked her, too," Carli admitted.

"Austin is terribly fond of her. She's been a heaven-sent angel of mercy in caring for him. I know she'd like to get to know you better."

"I'd like that, too," Carli said, understanding why when Gus had fled from hearth, home, and his wealthy family, he'd gone in search of "real people." She had developed a sudden appreciation for genuine, unpostured folks herself.

"I'd assumed that you would," Jasper said. "I took the liberty of contacting her, inquiring about her lunch hour scheduling, and I invited her to dine with us."

"Bless your heart!" Carli said, giving his forearm a fond and grateful touch. "Lunch is my treat, Uncle Jasper."

"If you insist."

"I do!"

"All I have to do is sign on the dotted line," Carli said.

There was a good feeling about having such freedom to do nice things for friends, even donate money to worthwhile charities, send help to the little church in Virginia. She knew that wealth was a blessing provided by the Lord, and that it was up to her to remember to be a good steward of the Dennis fortunes that had been presented to her by her husband.

As they rode in silence to the high-tone street where exclusive women's stores were located, Carli prayed that she would not lose her basic, decent, small-town values, that she would not have her head turned by riches, and that she would not end up paying a terrible price for the wealth that was now hers.

"This way, my dear," Jasper said as he led Carli into an elegant women's apparel store.

It was unlike any clothing business that Carli had ever shopped in. Immediately she was shown into a private, beautifully appointed area. Clothing was brought to her, as she was served coffee and refreshments. Salesclerks, who looked like socialites themselves, solicitously hovered around and offered expert advice.

Carli would have been dismayed at the time it took, except that she knew that Uncle Jasper was being pampered to an equal degree in the waiting area reserved for those who accompanied their clientele through the brass and plate-glass front doors.

"You'll look divine in all of these garments," the senior saleswoman assured.

"Is there anything else that you require?"

Carli knew that the purchases from lingerie to a new coat, would make a hefty mound on the counter as they rang up the ticket and carefully boxed the items for a deliveryman to place them in Uncle Jasper's trunk.

"Yes. . .I need something. . .for a funeral," Carli admitted.

"I'm sorry," the clerk said. "We'd heard Mr. Dennis wasn't at all well."

"Thank you," Carli said, her eyes tingling at the sincerity of the woman's sympathy.

"We have just the thing," she assured. "And in your size. . ."

eleven

Selecting appropriate clothing for a funeral cast a pall over Carli's morning. She was helplessly quiet as she signed the sales receipts and tucked the originals in one of her new purses. The salesgirl asked Carli if she preferred wearing the last outfit she'd selected prior to choosing a subdued, basic black, classic dress that would be appropriate for funerals.

"We can wrap up what you're wearing if you'd like to begin enjoying your purchases immediately," she offered.

"I'd like that," Carli decided.

Minutes later she stepped from the dressing room and rejoined Jasper, who arose from the wing-backed chair where he'd been reading a magazine.

"What do you think?" she inquired.

"Exquisite," he pronounced. "Very stylish. But without it destroying your own natural style. Becoming, indeed!"

"Thanks, Uncle Jasper. Do you think I need to do something about. . .my hair?"

"Absolutely not!" he stressed. "It's perfect the way it is. Many women wish they had such a crowning glory!"

"This was easier than I thought," Carli said as the store's delivery person stowed packages in the trunk of Jasper's BMW.

"I've enjoyed the morning." He glanced at his watch. "Now it's time for us to collect Sharon and have lunch."

When Jasper pulled into the parking lot he skirted the rows of vehicles and nosed into the staff parking lot adjacent to an employees' entrance. Minutes later Sharon Hathaway stepped outside, grinning and waving when she saw the pair waiting for her in Jasper's car.

"Where to, girls?" He asked after Sharon had piled in.

"We'll let Sharon choose," Carli invited. "Lunch is on the Dennises."

Although they could've gone to a fancy restaurant that Sharon might not have felt she could afford on a nurse's salary, she chose a quiet dining establishment known for its good food and a cozy ambiance conducive to intimate conversation.

Service was superb, the meal was succulent and flavorfully prepared to perfection. Conversation was as if the trio had been friends for years instead of a matter of a few days.

"What time do you have to return to work, Sharon?" Jasper inquired.

A light pink suffused her features.

"Actually, I don't have to return this afternoon. It's not every day that I make such entertaining lunch plans. Since I have plenty of personal leave accumulated, I decided to use a bit of it and put in for the afternoon off."

"Where I worked back in Virginia, we had to 'use it or lose it'."

"We can let it build," Sharon said. "Actually, we have a rather good benefit plan."

As they discussed such common, everyday topics, Carli realized how enjoyable the run-of-the-mill working girl chitchat was for her.

"Shall we return to the hospital and visit with Austin?" Jasper suggested. "Then if you two would like to slip away for awhile, I'll spend the afternoon with him."

"Sounds good to me," Sharon said. "I'd like to check in on him, even though I'm not on duty."

"Ditto!" Carli agreed.

The three returned to the hospital and progressed to Mr. Dennis's private ICU suite. Out of habit, Sharon Hathaway slipped behind the counter of the nurses' station and glanced over the staff's charting of the patient care given. She caught up with Jasper and Carli in the patient's room.

"How're you feeling this afternoon, Mr. Dennis?" She inquired in a bright tone. "I took the afternoon off, so I'm inquiring on a personal level instead of professional."

Austin Dennis produced a tired smile, but his eyes twinkled with enjoyment. "I'm hanging in there," he whispered.

"You just keep on keeping on," the nurse encouraged.

Jasper drew chairs closer to the hospital bed but Sharon and Carli carefully seated themselves on the edge of his bed. The frail and failing business tycoon seemed to enjoy the casual conversation that included him, even though he seldom spoke. Carli eventually realized that he was conserving his strength and breath for when Gus arrived from the office later on that afternoon.

"Do you want me to set the television channel for your usual afternoon programs, Aus?" Jasper asked.

"I'd appreciate it."

Jasper retrieved the remote control, pointed it at the television set secured to brackets high upon the wall, and pressed buttons that switched to a Christian channel.

"Mr. Dennis enjoys the good, old-time gospel music on some of the shows in the afternoon."

"It doesn't last long enough to suit me," he said in a feathery voice.

Just moments later the gospel hour came on. Carli could understand why Gus's father loved the programs, for it was foot-tapping, spirit-lifting, praise and glory hymns at their best. Carli found herself singing along. Then she stopped self-consciously when the three were looking at her instead of the professionals on television. Her lyrics trailed off.

"Don't stop," Austin coaxed. "I could listen to you all day."

"So could I!" Sharon said.

"Make it unanimous," Jasper chimed in.

By then the song had ended and a testimony begun.

"Carli and I have some plans for this afternoon, Mr. Dennis, so I'm going to borrow your daughter-in-law for awhile."

He nodded approval. "Just don't forget where you got her from. I know you'll bring her back."

"Sure thing."

Jasper started to search his pockets, apparently digging for keys to offer Sharon the use of his vehicle, but she dismissed him with a wave.

"My car's in the employees' lot," she said. "It may not be

as comfortable, but I'm accustomed to it, and we can slip around the city incognito."

"That appeals to me," Carli said.

"I thought it would."

"Have a good time, girls," Jasper said.

"You two gentlemen behave yourselves," Sharon teased, winking. "Don't cause the staff any problems."

"We wouldn't think of it!" Jasper gave a disdainful sniff, but one accompanied by a smile.

"That's Mitzi's domain, it seems," Austin Dennis weakly joked over what they all realized caused him a great deal of private pain and anguish.

Sharon Hathaway gently patted his frail shoulder, and Carli gave her father-in-law a light hug and a kiss on the cheek.

"We'll be back later," Carli promised. "Maybe Gus will be here by then."

"I'm really enjoying the day," Sharon said as they crossed the parking lot toward her car. "It's so different from my usual routine."

"I'm having fun, too."

"Bless Jasper Winthrop's kind heart. The whole congregation absolutely adores the fellow. He's so good and decent. Never puts on airs. He's signed up to periodically deliver Meals-On-Wheels to shut-ins, and he's as kind to an elderly charwoman as he'd be chivalrous to a countess."

"That sounds like Uncle Jasper. Is it far to your church?"

"Quite a little drive. But we'll swing by. We've nothing better to do. We can have a serendipitous jaunt around the area."

"I'd like that."

Sharon Hathaway expertly maneuvered her small car through the busy streets. Up ahead, several miles from the hospital, Carli saw a towering church spire that due to its location on a gently rising knoll seemed to dominate the older, semi-wealthy section of the city. When Sharon slowed and parked in front of the massive structure, Carli studied it.

Carefully manicured shrubs snugged the building, flanking

the wide steps that funneled worshippers up several tiers of steps and through the heavy wooden doors that looked as if they should have been complimented by a drawbridge and mote.

An elaborate masonry, iron and glass sign proclaimed the name of the church and worship information, but the angle of the sun caused a glare that prevented Carli from reading it.

"Is this where y'all go to services?" she asked, feeling a bit surprised to realize that such a huge church, which looked able to seat at least one thousand people at once, would possess the everyone-knows-everyone-else aspect of the caring Christian community that Sharon and Jasper had mentioned.

"Oh, heavens no!" Sharon corrected. She gave a hapless shrug. "This is where the Dennis family has attended services for the past several generations. I'm sure it's where burial services will be held. I thought you might appreciate, even need, a sneak preview. Jasper might be found acceptable to join this church's membership roster due to his long association with Dennis Mining and Manufacturing. They'd laugh me and most other working people right out into the boulevard if we chanced to appear, parking the cars we're making monthly payments toward fully owning next to their chauffeured limousines and foreign sports cars."

"Oh, dear. . ." Carli moaned softly. "It's a far cry from where Gus and I went to church in Virginia. We sang in the choir then. And several times Gus played the organ when the regular organist was unable to be present."

"There's no such volunteerism here," Sharon said. "They hire a music director with a master's degree, at the very least, and pay handsomely. Their choir is professional quality, too. They can afford to hire the best—so, of course, they do."

"That's sad," Carli said.

"And it discourages people from praising the Lord in music and in song."

"So much for thinking Gus and I might be part of the choir at this church," Carli said, realizing how sad that made her, for she'd clung to that hope as an area that would help to meld them together as the business world seemed to so easily threaten to rend them apart.

"We'd love to have you worship with us," Sharon invited. "When it comes to singing, the more the merrier!"

"That's how it was in the church where I was raised as a child. Anyone willing was welcome. I'll never forget one old, old woman, Mrs. Cornelius. Ethel was a mountain woman who was moved to town in her later years. She made the best corncob jelly in the county, God rest her soul, but she couldn't carry a tune in a bucket with a lid!"

Sharon gave a rich laugh.

"But she sang her heart out for the Lord, sometimes warbling off-key, terribly. But no one ever snickered, and after she passed on, the choir never seemed to sound quite as good to any of us."

"Corncob jelly, now that's a new one! Next thing you know, you'll be telling me you love grits!"

"As a matter of fact, I do!"

"I've never tried them."

"If you don't like them with butter and salt and pepper, then you're sure to find them appealing to your taste with butter, cream and sugar."

"You've convinced me to give 'em a try."

Sharon pulled away from the curb and time seemed to fly by as Carli told Sharon about her life growing up, her parents, and about her elderly aunts living in the sheltered care home in Nashville, Tennessee.

"I need to write to them and let them know where Gus and I are. We left in such a tremendous hurry that I didn't have time."

"Why write when you can call?" Sharon asked.

Carli paused. "I guess I didn't give it much thought. Gus and I were so used to budgeting our money, I suppose now I could."

"Of course you can. I happen to know that the Dennises have a WATS line at their residence."

"Thanks for the reminder. I'll do that tonight."

Once more Sharon parked in the street. The church wasn't

much more than a storefront on a street in a working-class neighborhood. Colorful banners hung in the window, and signs noted the times of services with words to effusively welcome any stranger to come worship with them.

"It's not a fancy church," Sharon said. "But it's got heart and life that many of the major religious institutions in this area haven't."

"I'll go with you sometime. Promise," Carli said. "Maybe Gus can, too. I know that he'll probably feel we should attend the church that's been his family's choice for decades."

"As good as you are, let us know in advance, Carli, and we'll make arrangements for you to witness to the congregation with your singing. You're good, you know that, girl?"

"So I've been told."

"Believe it, Carli. Believe it!"

It was much later, and the pair had stopped off for a cup of coffee before returning to the hospital.

Carli had appreciated Sharon as soon as she met her, but as the afternoon wore on, she knew that she also respected and trusted her. She found herself opening up about her confusing feelings and the odd sense of cultural shock and required adjustments that seemed to come too fast for an easy transition.

"You're doing fine, Carli," Sharon said. "And so is Mr. Dennis. Probably Gus, too, since you say he's a Christian. Mrs. Dennis is the person I'm concerned about."

"Oh?" Carli said, her eyebrows lifting as she sipped her cappuccino.

Sharon nodded solemnly. "We study a lot of things in nursing school," she explained. "We had countless clinicals. Not all of the clinicals dealt with the physical aspects of patient care. It's important that we help them make psychological adjustments, too, and deal with their emotional issues."

Carli admitted that she wasn't quite sure that she understood. Sharon sketched in the facets, some of which Carli had read about in magazines, such as the stages of grief experienced when a loved one dies or is facing imminent death.

"Oh. . .yes. . .now I know what you're talking about."

"Mrs. Dennis remains in a constant state of denial, only leaving denial to escalate into outbursts of anger, before she retreats into denial again."

"That makes sense," Carli said.

Already she'd concluded that Mitzi Dennis was acting as if her husband wasn't dying. Many wives, aware that their husbands wouldn't be with them much longer, would be spending every available moment creating lasting memories, reminiscing about the happiness of the past and what they'd accomplished in their lives together.

But not Mitzi Dennis.

She occupied herself with hair salon appointments, lunching with friends, attending social functions, going to the theater or concerts, availing herself of any number of amusements to occupy her life and busy her mind so that it was easier to blot from thought the fact that August Dennis, Jr., was dying of cancer.

Cancer specialists, including those from the Menniger Clinic, explained that further treatment would be unproductive, expensive, and only serve to diminish the quality of what life Austin had left before the Lord called him Home. But Mitzi refused to accept their verdicts, and instead she'd spent small fortunes arranging for treatments that were questionable, at best, and outright quackery and superstition at worst.

"Mrs. Dennis isn't an easy woman to like," Nurse Hathaway said, "but I love her and care for her as I do all people God wants for His children, even those who resist Him and scorn and persecute His followers."

"I know what you mean," Carli said.

Then, to her surprise, calmly, and dry-eyed, she told her about the conversation she'd overheard.

"We can pity her," Sharon said, "and we can pray for her, which we must do, and we can even love her in the sense of true *agape,* but don't be foolish and trust her."

"I've sensed that."

"As difficult and even dangerous as she is now, it might

become much, much worse when she's left a widow. She does care for Mr. Dennis, very deeply, and I fear what she might become like when he's no longer with us to serve as a. . . restraint."

"What do you mean, exactly?" Carli asked, even as a part of her sensed that she didn't want to know what promised to be an ugly and sordid truth.

"She might try to make Gus Dennis over into the image that she feels is appropriate for her son, and the man at the helm of Dennis Mining and Manufacturing."

"Oh. . .no."

"I know that no children ever have truly perfect child-hoods, but Gus may've had a particularly difficult one in ways that were not eased by the presence of money. Parental expectations are hard to ignore, my friend. And Mitzi Dennis is a powerful force with which to be reckoned."

"What am I going to do?"

"Gird yourself with the Scriptures, line up prayer partners, trust in the Lord, and rest on the reality that Mitzi Dennis and all that she represents are mere worldly, human power, and are weak and defeated in the Kingdom of God."

"I know that there are going to be difficult days ahead," Carli admitted.

"Comfort yourself that the tough times won't last one second longer than necessary for the Lord to work His perfect will. And that all things, no matter how ugly, hurtful, or heartbreaking, eventually work toward good for those who love the Lord."

"And we who love the Lord are many," Carli said.

"With more being added all the time, thank the Lord!"

"I'm so glad we got this chance to talk," Carli said.

"Anytime, Carli," Sharon invited. She produced a piece of notepaper from her purse and wrote her home phone number on it. "I'm there for you anytime, day or night. Remember that."

"I will. When it comes to a friend, Sharon, you'd be impossible to forget."

"It's time for us to return to the hospital," Sharon said. "I'd like to check on things before I head for my apartment. And we need to relieve Jasper for the day."

"With luck Gus will be there, or about to arrive, and I can get a ride home with him."

"Remember, I'm there, if he's unable to be there for you."

twelve

Jasper Winthrop had dozed off and Austin Dennis was resting comfortably when Carli and Sharon returned to the hospital and parted company at the elevator.

"I thought that Gus might've been here by now," Carli said, trying to hide her disappointment and the weariness she felt after such a busy and invigorating day following a less than restful night.

"He should be along presently."

"You can go home if you'd like, Uncle Jasper. You must be tired."

"I'll wait," he said, shifting in the occasional chair in the corner of the room to get more comfortable. "Gus and I can transfer your packages from my trunk to his car when he gets here."

"Right you are! I'd totally forgotten."

"You could call his office and see how long he'll be," Jasper said.

"I think I will," she said and retrieved the note card that Gus had given her from her purse. She quietly crossed to the telephone on the hospital bedside table and dialed for an outside line before she tapped in the sequence of numbers.

The Dennis Mining and Manufacturing switchboard operator took the call, and stated that Mr. Dennis was out for the remainder of the day. When Carli identified herself and asked about his whereabouts, the woman said she'd transfer the call to Gus's cellular telephone number.

Gus answered on the second ring.

"Hi, it's Carli," she greeted.

"Oh. . .Caroline, hi! Everything all right?"

"Fine. I'm at the hospital with Uncle Jasper. We were wondering when you'd be arriving."

"In just a few minutes. I'm two blocks away."

"Oh, okay! We'll meet you in the parking lot. His trunk is loaded with boxes containing my new wardrobe."

"I'll look for his car then," Gus agreed.

The pair donned coats and hurried from the private ICU suite while a nurse came in to help Mr. Dennis freshen up for his son's arrival.

Although it hadn't been easy for Carli to blithely sign her name and as a result spend the kind of money that the new clothes had cost, when she saw the way Gus's eyes lit up at the sight of her, and the approving glances he gave her outfit, she knew that it had been worth it.

"Have a nice day, honey?"

"Actually, very nice. Thanks to Uncle Jasper and Nurse Hathaway. We all did lunch."

"How nice."

"Sharon and I will get together again, even if it's only in the hospital cafeteria."

"Don't get so booked up that you don't have time to become acquainted with old family friends like Lauren Beekman. She dropped by and insisted on taking me to lunch today."

"How did things go at the office?" Carli quickly changed the subject.

"Rough, but everything went all right. It's given me an appreciation for what Dad did all those years."

"He bore a tremendous responsibility," Jasper said, "and paid a price, too, in terms aside from mere money."

"I can understand that. Perhaps this evening you can take it easy," Carli suggested.

Gus gave a bitter laugh that was more like a cough.

"Hardly," he said. "The more I figure out about it all, the more I realize I have to learn. I could scarcely fit all of the paperwork I need to go over by tomorrow morning into my briefcase. I'll have to plow into it right after dinner."

"It's been such a nice day that I hate to have it end. We've had so little time together, Gus, do you think we could go out for dinner on the way home?"

Actually, Carli wasn't terribly hungry, but she didn't wish to return to the Dennis mansion and have to suffer through the supper hour across the table from a critical and caustic-tongued Mitzi Dennis.

"Sure! Good idea, hon." Gus turned to Jasper. "Can you join us?"

"Thanks, but no thanks," the older man waved away the invitation. "You two need some uninterrupted time together without anyone else tagging along. I'll take a rain check."

"We'll hold you to that, Uncle Jasper," Gus warned. Then he checked his Rolex. "I guess I'll run up and see Dad."

"I've decided to take a light dinner at the hospital cafeteria rather than heat up something for myself at my apartment. Care to keep me company while I eat, Carli, so that Gus and Austin can have some privacy?"

"Love to," Carli agreed.

"That'll give me an opportunity to talk to you about an idea that's been rolling around in my mind all afternoon."

Jasper made his dinner selection, Carli chose a carton of orange juice, and they seated themselves off in a quiet corner of the cafeteria.

"I was wondering if you'd be agreeable to making a recording," Jasper began.

"What?" Carli blurted, confused by his question which seemed so out of context.

"Aus loves your singing. I know that if we'd make a record album, well, actually it'd be produced on cassette tapes or compact discs, of you singing old favorite gospel songs, that he'd cherish it dearly and listen to it as often as he's able."

"It's a nice idea, Uncle Jasper, and I'd be glad to do that for Gus's father, but the quality of singing into a tape recorder is tiresome to listen to."

"No—no! You misunderstand. It'd be professional quality."

"I don't understand, but what I gather is that you have to schedule time slots at recording studios, and that there's a lot of technical work, and expense. I doubt we've the time. . ."

"The mechanics are no problem, Carli."

Then Jasper Winthrop explained that several decades earlier Dennis Mining and Manufacturing had hired out all commercials made for radio, and later television, and the print media, but eventually they invested the funds in their own systems, and hired technicians on a per-job basis.

"There's a recording studio at headquarters," Jasper said, "and a call list of production technicians. It could be done right away. Tomorrow, in fact, and be ready quickly."

"I don't know. . ." Carli said.

"You saw how he enjoyed the programming this afternoon. The hymns seem to help him deal with the pain. Think what it could mean to him to have his favorite songs, sung by his favorite daughter-in-law—"

"His only daughter-in-law!" Carli interjected.

"—anytime he wanted to listen."

"Okay, you've convinced me," Carli said. "But I can't sing a capella."

"Don't you worry about a thing," Jasper said. "Leave the details to me!"

"Okay. Just tell me what to do."

"Be ready when I pick you up at eight-thirty tomorrow morning for a reading session at nine or whenever you feel warmed up and ready to cut your first record."

"I know you think I'm a good singer," Carli said. "But you're embarrassing me. I hope it won't turn out terribly."

"It'll be wonderful," Jasper assured, "and I have just the technician in mind we'll want to use. He can take the best— and make it even better."

That night Carli didn't say anything to Gus about Jasper's plans for her. When he asked where she'd like to dine, she named the restaurant that Sharon had selected.

"You do get around."

She shrugged. "The food's good. And the atmosphere is pleasant."

When they arrived, the manager recognized Carli and greeted her.

"It seems you're already winning over Boston," Gus mused. "Jasper. Nurse Hathaway. Now the manager here—"

"Everyone but your mother, and Lauren Beekman," Carli blurted before she could censor herself.

"Given time, honey, given time," he assured as he seemed

to caution patience.

Carli decided to leave well enough alone and say no more and instead questioned Gus about his day. He began to share with her in detail, although she didn't understand the half of it. She was just glad to be supportive on his behalf.

"Will you always have to work this hard?" Carli asked. "It seems that we hardly see each other."

"Mother used to complain that Dad was married to the business, not her. That was when I was a very small child. After a while she threw herself into her interests until her schedule was as jam-packed as his."

"We won't let that happen," Carli whispered.

"We may be helpless to prevent it for a while," he said, his tone somber. "Not only will it stay this hectic, but in the near future, it'll probably get worse. I'll have to travel."

"Oh. . ." Carli was helpless not to keep bleakness from her tone, especially at the idea of being left alone in the Dennis mansion with Mitzi Dennis and her loyal staff.

"Sometimes you can travel with me," Gus assured.

"That would be interesting."

Scarcely had they lingered over their coffee before Gus saw the time and seemed to jerk with alarm.

"This has been nice, honey, but we'd better get home. I have an awful lot of reading to do tonight."

"I wish I could do some of it for you."

He smiled and tousled the wavy full bangs that fluffed above her forehead and swept to the side. "I wish you could, too!"

At the mansion, Gus parked the car. Staunton met them at the door and assisted them with their coats.

"The keys are in the car, Staunton. The trunk's laden with packages. Would you retrieve them and remove them to Caroline's and my quarters?"

"Very good, sir."

"I'll be in the den," Gus said.

"I'll check in later in case there's anything you need for your comfort."

"You're a good man, Staunton."

"As are you, Mr. Dennis, as are you."

And with an uncharacteristic wink, one that was almost conspiratorial, the butler included Carli in the exchange. She couldn't help smiling. She had readily enough already fathomed the domestic situation. The Dennises lived in the mansion, but it was gentle, polite, courtly Staunton who actually ruled by pleasantly serving others, as Christ had long ago admonished in the Scriptures, that were as fitting in the present day as they were when He and His followers had walked on earth.

Carli thanked Staunton for delivering the packages. He'd offered his assistance, but Carli explained that she'd like to unpack and hang up the items herself. Then she planned to take a long and leisurely bubble bath in the sunken tub enhanced with whirlpool jets to soothe her tired muscles.

She'd laid her Bible on an ornate little tub-side table, adjusted a plastic-covered waterproof pillow to cushion her head, and began to read from the Good Book at random. Scriptures caused her heart to soar, and she prayed that tomorrow in the recording studio her voice could begin to do justice to the feelings in her soul and spirit.

thirteen

By the time Carli finished her bubble bath she thought about her aunts in Nashville, but realized it was too late at night to risk disturbing them even with the time zone difference.

One more thing to add to her to-do list for the next day, she realized, and experienced a stab of understanding for the stress and frustration Gus experienced in having too much to do and so little time in which to accomplish it all.

The warmth and soothing effects of the whirlpool bubble bath combined with the residual weariness reaming from sleep deficits accumulated the night before put Carli to sleep almost as soon as she slipped between the sheets and sank her head to the cool, comfortable pillow.

Aware that she had so many things to do come morning, she set the alarm on the bedside clock rather than impose on the household staff by asking someone to give her a wake-up call.

Carli had slept so soundly that it was as if she hadn't rolled over nor moved all night long so that when the unfamiliar buzzer sounded it jolted her awake with a start. It was at that moment that she realized Gus hadn't come to bed at all! His side of the mattress was untouched.

Hastily dressing, Carli left their quarters and slipped through the mansion that was just starting to come alive with the muffled sounds of servants leaving their rooms to begin the day. Even Staunton wasn't around to create the solid, ever-reliable presence he created.

Carli saw a shallow, thin slash of light emanating from the crack beneath the closed door to the den. She proceeded down the short hallway, considered knocking, but instead noiselessly turned the knob and eased the door open. The sight she saw melted her heart.

Poor Gus!

He'd fallen asleep in his father's massive, keenly expensive leather chair. The knot in his tie was loosened, his shirt collar askew, his cuffs unbuttoned and rolled back, his shirt rumpled. His reading glasses were loosely clasped in one hand, a pen scarcely gripped by fingers as he slept the sleep of one exhausted and borne down by the weight of the world and the crushing responsibility that was now his.

For a moment Gus's smooth, unlined face, muscles slack in sleep, reminded Carli of a little boy trying to fill his father's chair the way a spunky toddler might try. Right then Carli ached for what she knew he was going through, and realized how he had to feel terribly unprepared for all that was expected of him, and may have had moments, as did she, of wishing for his old comparatively stress-free job managing a pizzeria in rural Virginia.

Carli crossed to Gus and slipped her arms around him. He awoke with a jerk and blinked his eyes open.

"Gus. . .honey. . .wake up. . ."

"Oh, Car—Caroline. I guess I dropped off sometime during the night."

"Poor, tired Gus. . ."

"What time is it?"

"Time to get up," she said, and provided the exact hour.

He met the news with a ragged groan and forced himself to his feet, yawning.

"I think I hear a hot shower and fresh clothes calling my name," he said.

"That'll make you feel better. Some breakfast, too."

"I'll only have time for a cup of coffee. I have a breakfast meeting this morning anyway."

"Oh. Okay," Carli acknowledged, feeling disappointed that she wouldn't even have those brief minutes alone with her husband.

"It'll be a late night at the office. I'll be remaining after hours. So if you would like to make other plans—" he paused.

"Gus. . .is it always going to be like this?" Her tone was helplessly plaintive.

Gus gave her a quick kiss and a squeeze.

"Unfortunately, for a while at least. To be honest, honey, it'll probably get worse before it gets better."

Carli said nothing.

"I know that it's not easy," Gus said as they made their way upstairs. "Now I really understand what Dad meant over the years when he'd sigh and say that the family didn't own Dennis Mining and Manufacturing, it owned us. We possess the controlling stock shares, so we call the shots, and no one can make us do what we don't want to do with the company. But the fact is we're accountable to a lot of people—our stockholders—who've placed their trust in us. We can't let them down. A lot of widows and orphans rely on dividend payments from Dennis Mining and Manufacturing investments."

Carli was reminded of Aunts Eula Mae and Fanchon at the sheltered care home in Nashville, who lived more comfortably due to dividend checks from investments made in their younger years.

"With great wealth comes great responsibility," he pointed out.

"That's something I've begun to figure out. You pay a price when you have a lot of money."

Gus was so preoccupied in rushing to get ready to leave for the office that he didn't ask Carli about her plans for the day and she didn't volunteer information about the plans Jasper Winthrop had set in action.

A half an hour later, briefcase in hand, Gus quickly kissed Carli good-bye, and reminded her not to wait up for him.

Having only coffee and fruit for her morning repast, Carli was ready when Jasper came to pick her up.

"Ready to go record your first album?" He inquired.

"First, and I'm sure, my last," Carli said, laughing, "but yes."

"It'll be fun. Enjoy yourself."

"I plan to."

And she did.

The technician showed Carli around the company recording studio, explaining equipment to her, making it all sound much less complicated than she suspected it actually was.

Presently the musicians contracted for the day's work appeared, warmed up, and Carli did a few vocal exercises before she slipped into the booth, ready to begin.

Jasper had handed Carli music sheets for the repertoire of a dozen or so gospel hymns. It was comforting to have them in hand in case her memory momentarily caught over the lyrics although the songs were tenderly familiar from years of having been on her lips: "Amazing Grace," "The Old Rugged Cross," "Beyond the Sunset," "In the Garden," "You'll Never Walk Alone," "Peace in the Valley," "How Great Thou Art," and more.

Carli felt herself get into the spirit of the moment, the true spirit of God, and with chills rippling up and down her spine several times and goose bumps even peppering her skin from the depth of her emotional involvement, she was aware that never had she sung so beautifully nor poignantly majestically in her life. Instead of feeling tired when the recording session finished shortly before the noon hour, Carli felt rejuvenated.

"You're a natural," the technician said, his headphones hanging around his neck. His hands, which had flown over the control panel as he made various adjustments, were casually folded across his chest as he smiled at her.

"That's what I have been telling her," Jasper said.

"I never dreamed we'd do it all in one take after the initial run-through of the first cut for the album. You and the musicians are to be congratulated!"

"Thank you."

The technician turned back to the console that had made a soft sound as the system rewound. He retrieved a recording from the slot and snapped the metallic cassette into a protective container.

"I'll get this under production right away—within the hour. One of the best mix-men in the area had the day off today but I talked him into working for us this afternoon. Once he does his magic it'll be ready for duplication."

"Terrific!" Jasper said.

"How many copies do you want?"

One for Gus's father, Carli counted, one for Gus. Jasper would probably like one. She'd want one, of course, and it'd be neat to be able to send Aunts Fanchon and Eula Mae a recording, too. And maybe one for Pastor Meyer in Virginia.

"Five or six?" Carli suggested hopefully, as if she was fearful she might be turned down.

"Why not five hundred?" Jasper suggested to the technician, who nodded as if he believed that was a suitable and realistic number.

"No problem. None at all."

"You may as well have plenty, Carli," Jasper said. "Get them during the initial setup and production run. You'll want your children to be able to have copies, and someday even grandchildren."

"Oh. . .okay!" Carli quietly agreed.

She realized that Jasper assumed such a place of permanency for her, which she used to know, but hadn't experienced since they had journeyed to the Northeast and into Gus's past.

"There's a bonus in store if you can have a copy ready for Carli to present to the senior Mr. Dennis by three this afternoon."

"It'll be packaged and waiting," the technician promised.

"Fun, wasn't it?" Jasper seemed to almost tease Carli as they left the studio area of the business complex.

"It went so fast, it hardly seems it should be almost noon."

"You did quite a piece of work this morning, my dear. Hungry?"

"Ravenous."

"Let's see if Gus can join us for lunch," Jasper suggested.

"Another wonderful idea!"

Carli smiled at Dennis Mining and Manufacturing workers as she and Jasper Winthrop made their way through the plush corridors of the executive wing of the building. The way Jasper was greeted, Carli realized that even though he'd retired and was no longer on the Dennis Mining and Manufacturing payroll he still bore unquestioned authority and personal power when on the premises. Even so, he greeted everyone from top executives to mailroom clerks with equal warmth.

"Hello, Elizabeth!" Jasper greeted the older, very attractive and clearly competent executive secretary to Austin Dennis, and who now served his son.

"Jasper! How good to see you. You're looking well!"

"As are you," he replied. "We're here to see Gus."

"Go right in," she invited. "I'm sure that he'll be delighted by such a pleasant interruption."

As Jasper and Elizabeth had exchanged pleasantries the music on the CEO stereo system registered with Carli that it was different from the Muzak softly audible in the corridors and on the elevator. The music, strange, in a glaring, softly offensive manner, was discordant to Carli after having just recorded old gospel songs. It was unusual music with almost off-key harmonies, soft, lyrical chants, and foreign instruments that created tuneless melodies defying anyone's ability to hum along with such directionless passages. Yet, she found that the quietly jarring sounds were also subconsciously beguiling in an almost hypnotic manner.

Gus arose from his massive desk, smiling at the sight of the pair. "Well, hello! What a pleasant surprise to see you. . ."

"We stopped by to see if we could have lunch together," Jasper began.

For a moment Gus frowned. "Actually, I've already got a lunch date, but yes, sure! Sounds good! I know that Lauren won't mind, and would love to see you, Uncle Jasper. And this would be a great opportunity for Lauren and Caroline to get to know one another better."

At the news, Carli's heart sank. It plummeted even further when she scanned her husband's desk and took inventory of the items there. In addition to the trays of paperwork awaiting his attention and signature, there was a Dictaphone, multilined telephone system, personal computer, and on the corner, carefully removed from flammables, was a colorful arrangement of crystals nestled around an assortment of aromatic candles that were gently burning. Attached to the arrangement was a tiny card that was signed "Love, Lauren."

Carli realized the source of the odd music when she saw

the plastic, protective case for the compact disc that lazily revolved in the CD player. On the front cover were many odd symbols, and the picture of a white-clothed Hindu guru-type who had created meditative ashram variety music. A note from Mitzi assured him that combined with Lauren's New Age office-warming gift, and her own, he'd be empowered with all that he'd need to succeed in business and life.

Tears weren't far from the surface as Carli considered the bitter and brutal realities of life. As she'd been off in an adjacent wing of the building putting her heart and faith into making an inspired gospel album of songs that Jasper had whispered to her would "Sing Austin Dennis into the loving arms of Jesus. . ." in the office of CEO Gus Dennis twanged the strange stringed instruments that accompanied nasal, discordant, atonal nonmelodies among the heavy mystical odors of incense and specific "prescription" spices. Spices placed there by two powerful women, major influences for all of Gus's life, who seemed intent on collaborating to seduce Gus away from total faith in his Savior, and, Carli feared, away from fidelity to his lawfully wedded wife.

fourteen

When Lauren Beekman appeared to keep her lunch date with Gus, Mitzi Dennis was in her company.

"I ran into your mother at the Inner Journey New Age Book and Gift Shop," she rattled on. "Since we'd made a date for lunch I invited her to join us."

"I knew you wouldn't mind," Mitzi cooed, kissing her son's cheek as Lauren gave him a quick hug.

"I have guests, too, as it turns out," Gus said. "Caroline and Jasper will be accompanying us."

"The more the merrier," Lauren said and gave a twinkling grin, hugging Carli and Jasper.

"Great!" Mitzi chimed in, although Carli could tell that the older woman felt it was anything but terrific, although in seeing Carli's new, expensive clothing her chill eyes warmed a degree with grudging approval.

Although the food was wonderful, Carli had lost her appetite and she suffered through the meal, grateful that no one had inquired how Jasper and Carli had happened to be at Dennis Mining and Manufacturing's complex. And neither one explained their special mission, although in passing the time of day with the technician it had come to Carli's awareness that sometime Lauren Beekman had worked as a model and done a bit of community theater work and also had made commercials for various business, having gotten her start in that realm with the help of the Dennises who offered her exposure.

"We simply must get together again soon!" Lauren burbled on with what seemed false enthusiasm. "I know we're going to become the best of friends, Caroline."

"Caroline will have to act on the opportunity soon, darling," Mitzi reminded her young protégé. "You'll be very busy soon."

"I have quite a few travel plans. Palm Springs. Beverly Hills. Miami Beach. Las Vegas. Paris. . . Nice. . . The entire itinerary hasn't quite been solidified yet."

"Lauren has ever so many important friends," Mitzi said. "She knows just anybody who is anyone. She even has friends who'll send their private jets to collect her."

"How nice. . ." Carli said, feeling some comment was expected of her.

"I'll be qualifying for frequent flyer status myself before long," Gus said. "I've been postponing necessary trips to remain close to Dad. Until. . ."

"Flying! That reminds me," Mitzi veered away from the course the conversation was taking. "I picked up a little travel gift for you the other day. I hope you'll like it."

"And use it," Lauren added.

"Will you be visiting Dad this afternoon, Mother?" Gus asked, not to be deterred.

She seemed to frown over the fact that he'd mentioned the reality she was so desperately attempting to run from and forget.

"Not today." Her tone was blithe. "Probably tomorrow. I picked up what promises to be a wonderful book on reincarnation. I'd really like to read it right away."

Jasper Winthrop sat grim-faced and tight-lipped. Gus looked intensely uncomfortable, but hesitant in the face of his mother's fervor.

"I'll borrow it when you've finished it," Lauren put in a bid. "Do you want to read it first, Caroline? You might enjoy it. It'd give us something to discuss when we get together for lunch sometime."

"That's not my taste in reading," Carli said, aware that her voice was helplessly stiff and cold.

"She's into the Christian Bible," Mitzi explained.

"Oh, really? Well, there's a lot of wisdom in that, too," Lauren decided, as if the Bible was just an inspiring, man-made collection of stories and common sense, but not the inspired Word of God. She acted as if it were interchangeable with any of the New Age book titles that she and Gus's mother's bandied about, referring to the authors as regularly as believers did to the apostles who had recorded the Word of God.

"I find a belief in reincarnation very comforting," Mitzi said. "I like the concept. Especially now. . ."

"I find it appalling—and untrue!" Carli suddenly found herself speaking. "Not only that, but preposterous and ridiculous. As if the Lord Who created the heavens and the earth had to recycle souls!"

Lauren and Mitzi Dennis burst into sophisticated laughter as Jasper gave a rich chuckle and Gus was silent, aloof, distant and detached as if he'd suddenly been left devoid of all feeling for the emotional currents of the moment.

"Shall we go, dear?" Jasper suggested, cupping Carli's arm. "We've business to attend to," he reminded as he extricated her from a potentially volatile public scene.

Lauren and Mitzi accompanied Gus to the waiting limousine which would drop him back at the office, and Carli loathed that laughter which seemed to float across the parking lot after her.

Were they laughing over her "recycling" analogy, as Jasper had, or were they laughing, scornfully, at her most precious beliefs, her Lord, and her?

"The poor, deluded, spiritually blind women!" Jasper muttered, shaking his head sadly. "They're nettlesome and thoroughly irritating in their attitudes, but they're actually to be pitied."

"I know."

"Reincarnation, indeed!" he sniffed. "It seems that Mitzi Dennis has made up her mind that when she dies she's going to come back to earth in some form. I doubt she's considered that it'd be anything but that of a socially powerful wealthy woman. Who would want to cling to a deceitful concept like reincarnation if they'd studied the Bible and understood the unending joys of heaven?"

"I've never loved the knowledge of heaven or eternal security in the Lord more than I cherish it at this moment. I'm so grateful that my father-in-law is a believer. Such knowledge makes it all so much easier to face."

"The hopelessness Mitzi actually knows because of her pagan beliefs and hysterical seeking is what keeps her running away, especially now when Austin needs her, and prays to be able to witness to her and give testimony of the Lord, even if it's done with his dying breath. It's like there are forces influencing Mitzi to prevent any action, or willingness on her part, to allow that to happen."

At the realization, Carli was helpless to dab at a few gathering tears of sorrow.

"You just keep on praying, my dear," Jasper reminded. "And know that many prayer warriors are providing cover and support in the unseen realm. It'll be among the prayer requests at our midweek church services tonight."

"I appreciate that. I know others do, too."

Silence stretched. Carli's head ached. So did her heart. She wasn't sure which hurt worse.

"Would you like to attend services with me tonight? I'd be glad to pick you up. It'd be no trouble at all. I know it's short notice, but if you have no other plans and would like to—"

"I'd love to!"

"It won't interfere with Gus's plans?"

"Gus has plans. But I don't."

"Since you've nothing better to do—I'll pick you up—and will be delighted to have you present with us, as will Sharon Hathaway."

"No matter what a social agenda might contain," Carli mused, "nothing can compare with visiting the House of God and worshipping and fellowshipping with his people."

"Amen to that!"

Jasper left Carli in his BMW while he hurried into Dennis Mining and Manufacturing to pick up the finished cassette. To Carli's delight, he didn't have just one, but a small box, even shrink-wrapped, although the hastily computer typeset label was generic. Regardless, it was a thrilling moment for Carli.

Minutes later they entered the hospital and the elevator whisked them up to the private floor. Austin Dennis was up and alert when they entered his room.

"Carli has a surprise for you, Aus," Jasper said.

"A surprise?"

"Here!" she said, hugging him as she presented the cassette.

"I don't understand—"

Jasper explained and Carli was grateful to let him talk, unsure if she could trust herself to speak.

"Now your dear daughter's voice can be with you, singing your cherished hymns, my friend, day or night."

"I can listen 'round-the-clock," he whispered.

"I told her that it'd be she who would be singing you into the waiting arms of the Lord."

"Thank you," Austin said as tears filmed his cheeks. "Thank you both!"

Carli blinked fast, then was drawn into the old man's embrace as they hugged and softly wept together while Jasper wiped tears and patted their shoulders.

"We'll be parted," Austin said, "but I'll wait for you in Glory."

"Lord willing we'll all be there rejoicing forever around the Great White Throne."

❧

Two days later, headphones in place, as they had been whenever Austin had no visitors, he passed away as he slept with Jasper, Gus, Carli and a stricken, numb, even terrified-looking Mitzi looking on, seeming appalled and disgusted by death that had forever been the unavoidable destination for the living.

Mitzi had so gone to pieces with the knowledge that Austin was gone from her that she became hysterically overwrought. Gus tried to comfort her, but battling his own grief, it was too much for him, and he fled, blindly, from the room.

Exchanging glances, Jasper went after Gus while Carli was left to contend with the widow who was howling in a ragelike reaction to what all of her potions, crystals, and aromatic blends had not been able to halt.

Even though Mitzi had been purposely unpleasant, Carli's

heart broke on her behalf. When the weeping woman seemed to actually swoon toward her, Mitzi seemed to burrow into Carli's arms, as if trying to connect with some strength upon which she could draw, and seemed to find comfort and security in the touch of living flesh and blood. Carli's heart seemed to blossom with unconditional love, and swelled with the fervency of her prayers on Mitzi Dennis's behalf. There was hope in Carli's heart. She wondered if it would be a turning point for them, and if with Austin's death, a relationship of trust, love, even shared Christian faith, might become the shared family legacy. That was the prayer in Carli's spirit.

But within days, and after they'd moved through the routines of funeral preparations and grieving, she knew it was not to be. Mitzi had accepted her, even relied on her, in a moment of weakness. But it was clearly evident that her basic dislike of her son's wife had returned as strong and scornful as ever, seeming to be fired onward by the presence of psychics, channelers, rock stars, astrologers, and other entertainment industry people who were her New Age friends and had come to Boston from around the globe to pay respects and offer their weird explanations and grandiose philosophical words of supposed comfort.

Carli didn't know how much more she could take of the comings and goings of such strange people who were warmly welcomed to the Dennis mansion, while she continued to feel like an interloper. She admitted as much when Jasper took her to the airport to fly back to Virginia and wrap up their business and life so recently left behind there.

"Mitzi is in denial," Jasper said, "pretending that none of what's happened has actually taken place."

"I know," Carli replied in a bleak tone.

"Denial. An interesting, human reaction," he pondered. "People use it like self-administered Novocain to numb the body and the mind."

"I pray that the Lord will give me the strength to face and deal with reality and the grace to feel all the feelings and not try to escape into a pretend world instead of what's going on in my life."

"It's gotten bad, hasn't it?"

"I'm so fed up with Mitzi's pagan friends."

"She has her own travel plans. Certainly when she departs her residence the hangers-on will go elsewhere."

"Or else she'll take them with her."

"I wonder if she has a true friend among them all. She certainly picks up the tab all the time."

"I've wondered that myself."

"I don't want to come back if they're still here. I'm not sure I want to return anyway."

"Has it gotten that bad?"

"Yes. . ."

"How bad is it?"

"Bad enough that I'm fearful that my husband may be committing adultery with Lauren Beekman, although I pray not."

Jasper gasped. "Oh heavens—no!"

"And," Carli said, "I know he's cheating on the Lord. Mitzi bought him some silly crystal pendant attached to a neck chain that's supposed to keep him safe while flying. And when one of the psychics asked to see his palm—he let her—instead of refusing. Maybe he didn't want to offend his mother's friend, but it was offensive to the Lord. I'm afraid he's going to go along with the pagan shenanigans at the mansion and that he's going to end up buying into Lauren and Mitzi's claptrap."

"Likely he's only trying to placate Mitzi and keep peace. He's got to know better."

"Some of the people written about in Old Testament Scripture knew better, too, and got involved anyway."

"In the New Testament, too."

"Gus knows that the Lord is a jealous God, he wants all of Gus's adoration and commitment and worship and trust and faith. He won't tolerate sharing Gus with a heathen god! If Gus thinks he can keep peace with his mother he's actually foolishly going off to a battle, involved in a war without the Lord as his shield."

"Pray, Carli," Jasper soothed. "You'll have many believers praying with you. The Lord won't give up on Gus, even if it seems for a while that Gus is giving up on the Lord. The Lord's perfect will is that all would be saved."

"Those who are condemned stubbornly condemn themselves, I know, by rejecting and refusing salvation offered freely to those who believe in Christ Jesus."

"New Agers are tricky people, I've noticed," Jasper said. "While I was at the mansion quite a lot the week of the funeral, some of them were talking about 'The Christ Conscience.' It could fool someone if they didn't know that they weren't referring to Jesus, the Son of God, at all."

"Many good people are fooled and taken in. Pray God that Gus will not be one of them."

Carli's flight number was announced, even as she and Jasper seemed to both feel that they could've talked on at length.

"Godspeed, Carli, and God bless," Jasper said, hugging her good-bye and kissing her cheek. "This, too, shall pass," he reminded. "And remember that all things work toward good for those who love the Lord. Some people must have close brushes with true evil before they are willing to recognize and embrace the truth and goodness of the Lord."

Carli loved the Lord. Jasper loved the Lord. Sharon Hathaway loved the Lord. But did Gus? Time would tell. . .

fifteen

On her flight to Norfolk, where she'd rent a car to drive the remainder of the way to her final destination, Carli's mind played over the past month. The weeks following the funeral were difficult ones. Everyone in the mansion seemed to deal with their intense emotions and feelings of loss in a different way.

Jasper, by reminiscing about his longtime friend, fondly recalled events from the past and expressed readiness to go on and meet his friend in Glory when the Lord called him Home, too.

Carli had helped with writing thank-you notes and acknowledgments, listening to Jasper's stories, meeting Sharon for lunch and staying in touch with her old-maid aunts in the sheltered care home in Nashville. After their initial astonishment that Carli had married into the Dennis family from Boston, they adjusted to the unexpected news, as Carli had, and seemed to thoroughly enjoy the more frequent telephone calls and lengthy conversations. Carli would loved to have invited Eula Mae and Fanchon to come to Boston for a visit, and knew Gus wouldn't mind the amount spent on airfare, but there was no way that she was going to subject her dear aunts, who'd been little girls raised in a ramshackle cabin without indoor plumbing, to Mitzi Dennis's rude behavior.

For his part, Gus had thrown himself more fully into his work, using work like a numbing, addictive agent designed to keep him so busy, and so occupied, and feeling that he was making progress, so that he didn't have time to even think or reflect.

In the past Carli and Gus had gotten along well and enjoyed time together and had so many shared interests and easygoing personalities that they'd simply never argued, let alone spoken to one another in harsh tones. That had all changed now with cruelly edged words lacing their every conversation.

Mitzi, who had seemed at times almost catatonic in her numb detachment, and at other times when she was with her New Age friends almost hysterical in her beliefs, her demands, her need to control, manipulate, and try to convince others of the rightness of her constantly shifting philosophies, seemed to come alive in a perverse manner and take evil delight in the fact that Gus and Carli were squabbling.

It was a relief when Gus suggested to Carli that she fly down to Virginia to attend to their belongings, close out the apartment, and finish up business in what had been their first home.

Jasper had taken her to catch her flight mere hours after Gus had boarded another aircraft to fly out on an extended business trip. Since he would be returning home for only one day in the interim, he'd suggested that she take her time in Virginia and not time her return so that it coincided with his.

"You're sure?" She inquired, even though she had been very much looking forward to seeing old friends. "Real people," Gus had called them, and it was a definition she now understood and treasured, surrounded by people of such artifice as she was.

"Don't worry, darling. Mother—or Lauren—can take good care of me when I'm back in town and you're still away."

Carli had felt like giving in to a desire to present him with a sarcastic laugh, but it no longer took much to spark an argument and she was sick to death of fighting all the time. In recent days it seemed that few topics were. . .safe. Making no comment was!

When Carli unlocked the apartment door in Virginia she felt a rush of nostalgia for what had been. After resting up from the flight she set about sorting through the paltry accumulation of possessions. Some were discarded into the trash dumpster behind the apartment complex. Others were given to friends who were thrilled to receive useful cast-off items. Furniture was donated to a charitable organization that served the homeless and needy.

Carli turned over the title and keys to Gus's older car, at Gus's suggestion, for Pastor Meyer's wife to use to make it easier for her to keep up with her housekeeping and child care duties when the pastor had need to attend meetings, visit the sick, or make other pastoral duty calls.

Carli boxed up several containers of Gus's personal belongings and mementos and had them shipped to the Dennis mansion in Boston.

The items remaining from her own past seemed almost paltry, but in her eyes, precious. The picture albums bore photographic testament to strong Christian people who'd given her physical features, intellectual makeup, and a strong faith in the Lord. She held her parents' plain gold wedding bands. They had been too poor to afford a diamond ring, but knew in each other they'd found a perfect gem. The family Bible was well-worn. A few official documents and cards and letters saved over the years held special meaning to her.

There was Carli's high school yearbook from when she was a senior. She sat cross-legged on the floor and flipped through it, suddenly so homesick to be with people she'd grown up with who understood her.

She smiled as she confronted her own senior picture, and that of her classmates. They'd all felt so grown-up. But in reality, in looking at all of their pictures, she realized now how young, and innocent, and unworldly they had been.

She flipped through the pages. Many of the girls had gone on to be wives and mothers. Some were career-women. A few were already into second marriages.

A brochure from her fifth-year class reunion that she'd tucked into the yearbook slipped out onto her lap, along with a business card presented her by a classmate, Taylor Hayes, who, at their fifth-year reunion they'd congratulated because their senior year he'd been voted "Most Likely to Succeed." Tay seemed to be fulfilling their belief in him.

At that time he had signed on with a Nashville talent agency. His potential seemed to test the boundaries of the very galaxy. Carli could understand why. Taylor was smart, pleasant, he'd been good in the business classes they'd had together. He was also a very good singer, for they'd been in chorus together and had even sung duets a time or two at school and on several special occasions at the church they attended.

Recalling Taylor, she made a mental note to tell her aunts that the local-boy-made-good was in their midst in Nashville, Music City, USA.

Carefully Carli tucked her yearbook into the small suitcase, and then looked at the age-darkened, tan envelope that bore an accumulation of United States savings bonds her parents had purchased on her behalf over the years, which had been a nest egg that had given her comfort in the past, and now seemed to for the future.

The slow pace and friendly people in Virginia agreed with Carli, and she enjoyed visiting with former friends, gratefully accepting dinner invitations, but she sensed that there were some barriers that she was emotionally unable to tear down.

A part of her wanted to cry out and unburden herself and admit to her brothers and sisters in Christ about how awful her new life was in so many ways, and that wealth didn't bring happiness. There were problems that went away, she knew, by "throwing money at them," but even worse ones could appear to take the place of mere financial concerns and stresses found in working hard and trying to get ahead and make ends meet.

They all seemed to have an idyllic vision of what her life with Gus was now like, and she realized that in her own way she'd been convinced to become somewhat image-conscious and she was unable, through her own pride, to let the facade crumble.

She tried to play the role of the most content woman alive, and when they inquired after Gus, she explained him as being "busy, but just fine" and let it go at that. Such news seemed to make them happy, because it pleased them to believe that the man of wealth who'd been a blue-collar working man among them, had anonymously donated the furnace system, was being blessed indeed.

Carli felt that she was an actress and now the world was most certainly her stage. She felt that gradually she'd been swayed from recognizing the truth, facing it, and telling it until she'd become enmeshed in denying the realities that surrounded her which she'd concluded she'd be happier ignoring in order that she was not forced to confront and deal with them.

Only Pastor Meyer, it turned out, was not fooled. Carli realized this when, after dining with the Meyer family the night before she was scheduled to fly back to Boston, she found him scrutinizing her across the dinner table.

She was not surprised when he insisted, "You must see the new furnace system!"

Carli demurred, hoping to postpone what lay ahead, at least until she could collect her thoughts, but the pastor's wife was of no feminine assistance to her, for she cheerfully refused Carli's protests that it was only right that she help with the kitchen cleanup and dishes, and Carli had no choice but to dutifully follow Pastor Meyer the few steps to the church.

He sang the system's praises, explained the mechanical attributes which were lost on Carli, then he halted mid-sentence.

"As well as we know one another, Carli, we don't have to beat around the bush. I'll get right to the heart of the matter. I'm concerned about you. . .and about Gus. . .very, very concerned, in fact."

"Th–that's sweet of you—" Carli began with a careful phrase.

"It's not 'sweetness,' it's the heavy burden of knowledge given by the Lord that all is not well with you. In my spirit, Carli, I have an awareness that regardless of what your lips speak, or how cheerfully you may smile, things are not going well in your Christian walk through this fallen world. What's the problem? Perhaps I can help you to find and follow the Lord's wisdom."

For a moment Carli couldn't even speak. Then suddenly it was like there was no holding back as a cascade of emotions and feelings rushed over her like a tidal wave, tossing her here and there, all but drowning her in the swirling intensity that would not release her. First the tears came. Then sobbing words of explanation. She was helpless to withhold so much as one fact, not one solitary, sordid, scary detail.

"And my mother-in-law absolutely despises me," she cried, choking on her tears and the force of her words. "She's probably a good and decent person in her own way," Carli tried to soften the description of the source of her deepest hurts and public humiliations. "But a part of her, the way she is, and how she defies the ways of God and scorns the Lord and His people who love Him. . .it's like there's something dark about her. Something truly evil! An–and it's like with her power, influence and ability to pressure, and manipulate and shame and cajole Gus that he's being brainwashed."

Pastor Meyer was silent a moment.

"Brainwashed. He is being brainwashed," he softly pointed out. "That's how cults and New Age belief systems work and how they get converts to their fraudulent, foolish, fanatical ideas."

"What am I going to do?" Carli beseeched. "At one time I believed that where Gus went, I would follow him. But," she admitted bitterly, "I'm no Ruth. . .!"

"Nor is your mother-in-law a Naomi, apparently."

"And Gus is no Boaz, either! I don't know what to do. I'm so confused."

"I don't know what you should do, Carli, but I do know that the Lord has a perfect plan for you. . .for Gus. . .for his mother. . .and this other young woman whom you fear is seeking your husband's affections. I know that marriage is a permanent, sacred bond, a vow given not only to one another, but to the Lord. I do not believe in divorce. . ."

"I don't, either, but I don't know how much more I can take. It's starting to grind away at me, wear me down, and affect my Christian life. Not for the better, that's for certain."

"I had noticed a few changes. I'm thankful you're aware of them," he said gently.

"I can't let being surrounded by human beings alter my

relationship with the Lord. Frankly, I'm about ready to shake the dust off my feet and move on where Gus's family and his mother's friends are involved!"

"You may have to one day take such drastic steps. Divorce isn't the answer, but sometimes a wedded state of separation can be healing. It allows the space within the sanctity of honoring the marriage vows, for the couple to leave the sources of pain and frustration and present wounds so that they can begin to heal, think clearly, and reach conclusions without being under the influence of inflamed emotions or get-even tactics. It offers a chance to begin to miss one another, to recall the good times, and want to regain those earlier feelings. It also gives the Lord a chance to transform lives, as the separated couple is more likely to hear the Voice of God speaking to their hearts if they're not busy shouting one another down."

Carli couldn't help smiling. How succinctly he'd summed it all up. She realized that it wasn't the first time he'd offered such counsel, it wouldn't be the last, and in her heart she knew it was a true and workable solution that on her own would be insurmountable.

"Maybe there's hope after all."

"Of course there is. And if Gus were here, I'd tell him to get a dwelling for just the two of you, even if it was above a laundromat, because I know that nowadays there's no house big enough to contain a man's wife and the young woman's mother-in-law."

"A forty-eight room mansion makes a two-room efficiency seem very appealing, believe me."

"It'll work out," Pastor Meyer assured as he gently touched her forearm. "You and Gus are continually in our prayers. And rest assured that that will not change."

"Thank you."

"If the day should come when you decide you must leave and live the life of a separated married woman to resist forfeiting fidelity to your faith, you're always welcome in this town, and would be among friends and Christian brothers and sisters."

"That's comforting to know," Carli said, even as in her heart of hearts she knew that it would never be, for it was a place of so many haunting memories. . . .

sixteen

Feeling stronger, Carli returned to Boston with renewed hope, determination, and confidence, hopeful from what Pastor Meyer had said. Perhaps absence would make the hearts grow fonder and a brief parting would improve their relationship. Within forty-eight hours she discovered that it was not to be. In fact, matters seemed much, much worse!

Upon returning home, hours after Gus, too, flew in to Logan International Airport, rather than to expect Staunton to go through garments and prepare them to be deposited in the dry cleaner's pickup bag when the van arrived, Carli attended to the duties herself. In the inner, silk-lined breast pocket of one of Gus's suits, her fingertips collided with something stiff and she discovered a postal card and retrieved it from its place of safekeeping.

"Gus Darling," it read. "I loved our out-of-town rendezvous. It was as if we'd never been parted by all those many years when I missed you so dreadfully. I'm so glad that our travel itineraries meshed for this little interlude. I'll keep you apprised of my travels and hopefully our paths will cross on a regular basis. Thank you for your personal presence in my life again. Words fail to satisfactorily convey my fondness and appreciation for all that you've done for me and mean to me. Dennis Mining and Manufacturing has been good to me, and I consider The Mansion a home away from home. I spend hours meditating on the future I want to be mine and channel all of my psychic and physical energies in that direction. My love—Lauren."

Carli's heart froze.

What did it all mean? She wondered long minutes, but wasn't sure what the innuendoes suggested, but deep within she had the ominous sensations that none of it boded well for her. . .or Gus.

Two hours later, her unease was confirmed with unimpeachable evidence and realities that were impossible to deny and ignore.

Carli had gone downstairs and Staunton announced that the route letter carrier for their area of Boston had just dropped the day's delivery through the metal mail slot cut in the door.

Staunton had further separated it into individual stacks for all of those for whom the Dennis residence served as their mailing address.

Mail for Mitzi was stacked in her pigeonhole of an ornate brass and glass slotted cabinet affixed to the wall above the foyer table. Mitzi had been gone since the day after Gus had flown out of town on business while Carli was still in Virginia. This time, Carli believed, she'd jaunted off to Mexico, with one of her many friends, and they were going to vacation in the nation's coastal area that was a region of sunny, white beaches, palm trees, and the beguiling blue of the Pacific Ocean. Beachfront villas, the surrounding air heavy with the scent of bougainvillaea and other tropical flora and fauna, were easily rented by the wealthy who could afford the fees.

It was also a shopper's paradise for those who braved the native markets looking for curios, handmade items, and unusual crafts that the local peoples peddled to support their impoverished families.

It was also a New Age buffet of beliefs and practices, and self-proclaimed, or area-recognized, adherents who were hailed as experts in their paranormal fields, and were willing to indoctrinate, educate, and train others—especially wealthy gringos—who were interested in acquiring strange knowledge through their occult dabblings.

It frequently took Mitzi a full day to go through her mail when she arrived home. Staunton placed the first-class mail in her large pigeonhole in the mail repository, but the magazines and newspapers to which she subscribed, as well as monthly selections for New Age book clubs to which she belonged, were packed away in a wicker chest that with its innocent appearance, didn't look to contain what Carli considered dark, depraved, even demonic materials.

Rarely was there anything for Carli, and that was to be expected. She hadn't been in the Boston area long enough for her status as Mrs. Austin Dennis III to be on numerous direct mail solicitations sent to potential customers. Except for an occasional card or clipping from her aunts, who subscribed to the old hometown newspaper and sent her items of interest, she had little mail.

Therefore, she was surprised to find that in the slot for her was a chunky, neatly wrapped little box, like that which might contain a paperback book, addressed to her, but with no return address. The typeface seemed computer generated on an unremarkable self-stick label, and she wondered if it was some kind of get-rich-quick marketing video or book, or some other uninvited sales attempt to involve her in a project or charity.

A little white peel-and-stick label at the lower left stated: *PERSONAL. YOUR IMMEDIATE ATTENTION AND RESPONSE ARE REQUIRED.* She smiled. She'd seen that before, too, as direct mail promoters using bulk rate mailings attempted to have their printed materials resemble higher-priced special delivery type envelopes in order to cause occupants who surveyed them at a glance to take them more seriously.

She slit the cardboard with the ivory handled letter opener nearby. She almost broke a fingernail trying to get what was obviously a videotape out of the snug box, then finally freed it. There was no label, nothing, just the ominous typed message for her to watch the video right away, and not to postpone action.

Only because she really had nothing pressing to do, and she realized that if she viewed it, then she could in good conscience toss the material away and be done with dealing with the delivery, she went to their quarters. She could have gone to the TV in the den, which was a large-screen set, but she'd already decided to spend the afternoon reading, writing, napping, and then perhaps seeing if Jasper or Sharon was free to dine out with her.

Expecting the video to be some kind of sales presentation, perhaps gorgeous scenes from a land that a travel agency would like to interest her in visiting, Carli shoved the slot into the video cassette recorder and pushed the play button.

The VCR hummed softly, then the lead-tape was through and it was a moment before images came into shape, and the recorded voices were audible.

Carli stared, horrified.

"Oh. . .no!" she whimpered.

Tears stung her eyes.

There on the screen were images, as if the haunting and hurtful suspicions that had returned time and again to plague her thoughts had somehow been transferred to the tape in the video.

The action on the screen was mild compared to some of Carli's worst suspicions, but she knew where such mild beginnings led, and she ejected the cassette, angrily flinging it across the room, then threw herself on the bed and wept and wept until it seemed as if there were no more tears left. But still they continued to burn a hot train down her cheeks that seemed to burn to the depth of her very soul.

Who wanted her to be faced with the ugly reality and pushed out of the way by her hurt pride and helplessness to forgive and forget and go on?

Gus, who wanted his freedom and the old life that had been planned for him since babyhood?

Lauren, who'd informed Carli on sight that she "hated" her, and seemed to consider Gus someone stolen from her, the poor little rich girl who had everything her heart could desire. . .except for Carli's husband.

Or was her mother-in-law aware of what was going on, knowing it was the kind of proof that it would be nigh on impossible for Carli to ignore.

Was it someone at Dennis Mining and Manufacturing. . . who felt that the wife was so often the last to know, and this person didn't like to know others were making a fool of an unsophisticated country girl?

Who. . . ?

WHO?!

Carli didn't know. She realized she didn't even care.

There was no returning to the state of innocence she'd been able to believe in as recently as an hour earlier because now the random thoughts in her mind weren't just supposition and groundless conjecture.

Carli was grateful that she had informed the kitchen staff she would be dining out and given them freedom from any evening duties. Now, she was extremely relieved that to a one they'd made quick arrangements to spend the evening away in pursuit of their own relaxation and interests.

She was doubly grateful that she'd presented the same offer to Staunton, when he'd been nearby when she'd retrieved her day's mail, because although he'd looked as if he felt he should remain on scheduled duty, a part of him wished to enjoy an unanticipated evening to do whatever he wanted.

A half an hour later, Staunton tapped on the closed door to Carli's room.

"Are you certain you won't require my services this evening, Miss Caroline? I'm most willing to remain if you think that you should have any need for me to be present on the premises."

Carli strained to make certain that her voice carried no hint of her inner turmoil and that it had the right tone of carefree casual pleasantness that she wished to convey.

"No need, thanks. Run along and enjoy your evening. Don't concern yourself with me, Staunton. I can safely see myself in and out this evening."

"As you wish," he agreed. "And thank you, Carli."

"You're welcome!" she sang out even as her heart seemed to break. "Enjoy yourself!"

A short while later she heard the sound of the engine of his car. She arose and watched it progress down the street, feeling somewhat amazed when she looked down, dazed, as if another had taken control of her thoughts and mind, and realized that she was sadly waving after the kind, compassionate, concerned, and caring butler as he departed. . .as if she might never see him again.

With the awareness that she was alone, all alone, in the Dennis mansion, Carli flew into action. She retrieved her old suitcase that no one had ever discovered and discarded as unworthy of the new Mrs. Dennis, and she transferred her keepsakes that she'd brought back from Virginia into it.

Then she reached into the back of her closet for the garments that the saleswoman at the exclusive women's store had boxed and wrapped up for their return home in order that she could appear on the street in her newly purchased garments.

She went to the jewelry box Gus had given her and she stripped off the expensive watch, the expensive jewelry items, and tucked them into the velvet-lined container. She wrenched off the large, gaudy three-carat solitaire diamond ring that had no meaning to her, although its size and cost seemed to have mattered to Gus.

She pushed it into the slit between stuffed rows of velvet-lined material to safely contain rings, and retrieved the tiny ring that had been blessed as a symbol of their sacred vows to each other and to the Lord. She slid it on her finger.

She emptied the contents of her expensive purse into the one she'd possessed when she had arrived in Boston and exchanged her elegant, expensive coat and shoes for those which had been modestly priced but served her well.

She looked around the room. There was so little she desired to take. Almost nothing of Carli Dennis—the real Carli Dennis—had made any impression on the room, let alone the length and breadth of the mansion and the Dennis compound.

Carli went downstairs after carefully hanging a "Do Not Disturb" sign on the outer handle of the doorknob, locked it from the inside after herself, knowing that Staunton could open it easily enough when the alarm was raised and there was deemed a need to investigate.

By then, she would be far, far away.

The last act that Carli did before she closed and lock the door of the ominously empty Dennis mansion behind her was to open the Yellow Pages, telephone a taxi company—

the first one whose ad caught her eye—and summon them to the address of the Dennis mansion.

She was waiting at the curb, suitcase in hand, when the taxicab arrived at the gate.

"Where to, Ma'am?" the cabby inquired.

Carli gave the name of a bank, and then during the ride checked her wallet to make sure that she had all of the identification necessary to cash in the United States savings bonds that would fund her in her desperate escape from such unhappiness and the twining world of New Age, infidelity, and dark emotions that threatened to ensnare and strangle her existence as a human being and a child of God.

Carli dismissed the cabby, tipping him, confident that she could hail another taxi as soon as she departed the financial institution.

Fifteen minutes later, she did so, and asked the driver to take her to Logan International Airport.

He let her out in front of the terminal.

As her afternoon had progressed, Carli hadn't been too certain of what she was going to do, where she was going to go, but the call of blood—the need for family—had been an insistent hum in her very veins. She had to go to her people. And, as she set about to do so, she better understood Gus's need to return to home, hearth, and the ways of his raising. He'd done it and destroyed her life—now she was doing it in hope that it would be the protection of her salvation.

Carli almost wilted with relief to discover that there was a flight leaving for Nashville, Tennessee, within two hours, and that there were seats available.

"I'll take one, please," she said, and paid for the ticket with cash, using her identification as Caroline Waggoner to book the ticket.

With time to kill, she considered that Carli Waggoner's money could soon run out, and that the travel expenses that the new Mrs. Austin Dennis III wouldn't have batted an eyelash over would paralyze and soon impoverish Carli Waggoner.

She was going to have to get a job—and fast. With a bit of

time to kill, and aware of the time zone difference, Carli went to the bank of telephones. She carefully sorted through her possessions until she found her high school yearbook, the newsletter and then the business card that Taylor Hayes had passed out to the classmates he'd visited with so warmly, inviting them to look him up anytime they were in Nashville.

Carli, who'd known Tay better than a lot of classmates, knew that it hadn't been the egotistical actions of someone who wanted to play the big shot and show off over his position in the entertainment industry. She knew that he'd meant it—and that is what gave her courage to dial the number on the expensive card.

She'd expected that it might be almost impossible to get through to him. But saying a quick prayer that the call would be quick and not eat up pay phone funds faster than she could afford to squander them, she put the call through.

As she had suspected, a switchboard operator took the call.

She asked to speak to Taylor Hayes, was connected to his receptionist, asked if she might speak to him, and when the office worker asked her identity, she explained, "Carli Waggoner. We went to school together back in Kentucky—"

She was ready to offer promises that she wasn't a hopeful entertainer or some persistent hanger-on, or entertainment industry want-to-be in hopes of acquiring a moment's time. She was not prepared for the receptionist's response.

"I'll put you right through, Ms. Waggoner. He's been expecting that you'd call—"

Hoping she'd call? But why? Did the receptionist have her confused with someone else? Little matter what the circumstances, she'd been put right through to Taylor, who she hoped would be happy hearing from her, considering all of their shared memories created during their growing up years.

A moment later he was on the line, elation in his tone clear.

"I'm coming to Nashville, Tay, so, of course, I'm looking you up first. . ."

"Well, I should hope that you would!" he said, laughing easily.

"I'll have to go to work soon."

"No problem there, Carli. You've got a slot here with Rising Star Talent Agency if you're willing to sign on."

Her heart soared with relief. Clearly he recalled how well she'd done in office procedure classes in high school and was aware that she was a dedicated, honest, efficient worker, so that she would be considered an asset to the firm.

"How soon are you going to be arriving?"

"Within a matter of hours."

"When you decide to act on something, you don't waste time. This is great! What time's your flight going to be in?" Carli told him. "I'll either meet you at the airport," he said. "Or I'll have one of my assistants, Paige or Loralee, be there to pick you up."

"How thoughtful," Carli cried with gratitude.

"We treat our people right here," Taylor assured, and Carli considered that compared to the chilly reserve of the Yankee Northeast, the slower-paced, Southern warmth was exactly what she required. "You'll need a place to stay?"

"Yes. . ." Carli was about to say that she'd get a room at an inexpensive hotel, but Tay spoke before she could.

"I can take care of that, too," he said in a blithe tone.

Carli's thoughts spiraled until she felt almost dizzy. Was he insinuating that—? Had he changed from the small-town youth she'd remembered who shared faith and ethics identical to hers?

Then he spoke on, and Carli almost sagged with relief to realize that she had been wrong. Tay had grown up and matured but he was basically unchanged.

"We handle a client who's on tour in Europe," he said. "She has a nice apartment. She asked me to sublet it. We have some people interested, but I haven't gotten around to having interviews done to choose someone to sublet. If you want the place, Carli, it's yours. The price will be right—and it has everything it needs. Everything but an occupant."

"I'll take it!" Carli said, relieved. "Listen, Tay, I know you're busy, and I'd better go. I'm at a pay phone and don't want to end up owing the company from one call."

"We'll talk this evening."

"Great."

"And thanks for choosing to call me, Carli. I know you didn't have to and I really, really appreciate that you did."

"You're welcome."

"Don't have more than a holdover bite on the flight, Carli," Tay admonished. "I have some surprise plans for this evening."

"Knowing you, it'll be an evening to remember."

"I think you'll enjoy yourself."

"Until then," Carli said. "See you in a few hours!"

"Enjoy flight level at thirty thousand feet, Carli, because while I know you're a girl who has her feet on the ground, and one who's heavenbound some day, from now on you're on the launch pad. You do your part—we'll do the rest!"

For her part, she'd had enough of high society and the stratospheric levels of living that required. She was now leaving that behind her.

She loved Gus. She would always love Gus. For her part, she would forever be his wife unless he chose differently and divorced her in an action that she realized she would not contest if that was his desire. Regardless of that realization of potentialities, especially with the fleet of lawyers retained by Dennis Mining and Manufacturing to get rid of her if he wanted to, she prayed that their marriage could be healed, his faith preserved, a future together restored.

But she was aware that it would take the Lord's intervention to accomplish this, and Gus was no longer a godly person, and was too solidly influenced by his flighty, frivolous, foolish, New Age follower mother and her cute, charming, convivial, and clever young protégée, Lauren.

Feeling like a wounded animal, leaving its home, seeking a quiet, hideaway location in which to lick its wounds and gain strength, or else a place to serenely and privately die, Carli boarded the airplane for Nashville and looked forward to the evening in a new apartment, and the opportunity to job hunt in the morning, and then the following afternoon, drop in to announce herself and tell her startled, surprised aunts hello!

seventeen

It was a sad walk for Carli to wend her way to the boarding gate to depart on her Nashville-bound flight. There was no one to whom she'd offered an official good-bye. She knew that she would contact Jasper and Sharon, to assure them that she was fine and ask that they not worry about her whereabouts or her welfare, and that she would keep up the relationships from her end when she had laid the foundation for a new life.

The sad truth was that her marriage had been one in name only almost since she and Gus had returned to Boston. Now she was a runaway wife. Upon either rashly, or with forethought, choosing to flee, runaways seldom informed those they were leaving behind of a departure destination. She hadn't exactly hidden her actions. If Gus wanted her back. . .she knew that in a matter of hours he could have a professional track her down due to the computer data that marked her trail. At the moment, as far as Carli was concerned, the next move was entirely up to him.

Carli felt wilted by the time the flight attendant processed everyone and they went into the preparation for the take-off routine. Because Carli was traveling light she stowed her carry-on suitcase in the compartment overhead. Although she could have cordially visited with a seat partner, had one been assigned for the flight, she was grateful it was vacant, for it afforded her the time and opportunity to think and to pray.

Exhausted from the emotions that she'd experienced, Carli would liked to have dozed on the flight to Nashville, but her mind was on overload with all that had taken place. And, there was the niggling sensation, too, that somehow, in some strange way, it had been as if her conversation with her lifetime friend, Tay Hayes, had been as if she was describing oranges, and he was talking apples. She couldn't quite put her finger on exactly what unidentifiable spoken overtones had faintly put her on guard, and she prayed that it was just her anxiety about it all that made her feel as if there was potential for misunderstanding.

She wanted him for a friend, that was all, and she'd been hoping—counting on—Hayes to give her a letter of recommendation, which, coupled with her resume could open doors to quick employment. But it had sounded very much as if she would have a job awaiting her, all she had to do was officially agree to work for the Rising Star Talent Agency and there was a position to claim. She knew she was a good worker, and wouldn't disappoint anyone in her abilities, but she wondered at Tay's quick offer of a job. Did he have a private agenda he was following in doing so?

Tay hadn't dated much in high school, nor had she, and while they'd cherished one another's friendships, neither had ever tried, nor seemed to want, it to become much, much more. She still felt that way. But had Taylor's views changed? Was he actually attracted to her but knowing her so well was aware that he'd have to move slowly to avoid alarming her? Did he want her working for the firm where he was employed so that she'd be conveniently close by?

Softly groaning, feeling irked with herself that her thoughts were wandering such emotionally charged circuitry, she forced her reflections away from such, what had to be, absurd, even embarrassing considerations if Tay ever knew she'd thought such a thing that he might be attracted to her.

In what seemed almost no time the pilot's voice came across the intercommunications system with the time that was accurate for the area, pointing out famous landmarks in Music City USA and joked that they would be landing at Nashville International Airport and not the John C. Tune Airport. At first Carli thought he was making a Music City related joke before she realized that there were other airports in the city, and one had a music-related title.

She fetched her baggage, then made her way into the terminal. She scanned the waiting persons, then a woman, slim, tanned, beautifully and attractively groomed, who wore an outfit that could only be considered "power dressing," called out her name.

"Hi!" she said. "I'm Paige Logan. You must be Carli Waggoner."

"That's right."

"You haven't changed much from the picture Taylor showed us this week from your old high school yearbook."

"Oh, really?" Carli commented, suddenly feeling major concern.

What was a man like Taylor Hayes doing keeping his old high school yearbook at the office? And what on earth was he doing showing her picture to his staff days before she'd had any idea that she'd be fleeing to Tennessee?

Paige seemed not to notice that Carli was quietly reflective, and appeared to chalk it up to jet lag.

"We'll have to hurry. We need to get right back to the Agency complex. Grab a quick peek at landmarks as we go past them," Paige said. "I'll give you a more leisurely tour when time isn't so crucial."

"Okay," Carli agreed. "So what do you do?" She asked, wanting to get the Rising Star Talent Agency's employee to break the threatening silence with her informative, interesting chatter that was delivered in a warm honeyed tone so soothing to Carli's ears and outlook.

"We're here!" Paige announced, wheeling into a slot that had a discreet marker that informed everyone it was her personal parking space, which was located near the entrance, but not so close as others who were obviously located further up in the power structure of the agency hierarchy.

"Leave your things in the car," Paige said. "We can swing into the ladies' room off the lobby if you'd like to take a minute or two in order to freshen up before we head for the big meeting."

Carli had assumed that Paige meant "meeting," as in a definition for "reunion," for it had been two years since she'd last seen Tay at their class reunion.

After exiting the luxurious area, brushing her hair, tracing on fresh lipstick, applying a quick spritz of perfume and making sure that her clothing was in order, she and Paige headed down the corridors that were every bit as elegant and expensively furnished as had been the Dennis mansion.

Tay arose, crossing the room at the sight of her.

"Carli Waggoner! You look ravishing!" he said. Tay took her hand, gave her a quick squeeze as he slipped his arm around her shoulder, and seemed to pivot her to face inward into what was a long room, where Tay had been seated at the head of what Carli came into sudden focus to recognize as a board meeting.

Her face flamed with alarm that Paige had ushered her into a private, high-level corporate meeting, when the matter of a reunion with a person from Taylor's personal life could have been postponed until a more convenient moment.

And, Carli was certain, it didn't require a meeting of the top brass and upper echelon power brokers to employ another individual to help with datakeeping and office routine duties.

"This is the newcomer I've been telling you about," Taylor began an introduction. "She's an old friend of mine from back home in Kentucky."

Due to her recent indoctrination into the ways of the Dennises, Carli was aware that she made a presentable social response, although she was inwardly caught terribly off guard. Her confusion was complete when Tay seemed to call some kind of meeting to order.

"In case y'all haven't had a chance to listen to the demo tapes that I had delivered to you by messenger earlier in the week, I'll give it a quick play now."

Carli felt excitement at the prospect of listening to an actual demo tape, that she might compare it with what Jasper Winthrop had had produced. She felt as if she was hallucinating, and it was almost horrifying, when she recognized her voice and her songs emanating from the top-of-the-line, state-of-the-art equipment.

Carli said nothing. Nor did anyone else. They were listening intently. It was as if the shock had struck her senseless.

How? What? Why? Who?

Unfinished questions jumbled and tumbled through her mind with Carli unable to provide even the beginnings of a semblance of an answer to any of it. Once again she knew the discomfiting sensation of having walked into a movie late, and everyone knew exactly what was going on, except she.

"As you all know, from the letter that I sent along with the cassette, which was hand-delivered by a courier-service, I've been acquainted with the aunts of Ms. Waggoner since the day I was born, and I visited them recently at their residence in Nashville. They played a recent professional quality tape made by their niece. I listened to it, they allowed me to borrow their copy, and the rest is history."

History? Carli had no idea what was going on. But everyone was talking as if somehow it was cut and dried.

"I posted a letter to Carli asking her to come to Nashville, and, apparently, as soon as she got the invitation, she made up her mind, for she called to announce her intentions to come here."

Letter? What letter?

Carli wasn't going to interrupt what Tay was saying, but in her mind she did quick calculations and realized that had Taylor given it thought, he'd have known that even with overnight mail services, she had called him before she'd had time to receive written communication. It had been a strange turn of events, and bit by bit, the mysterious puzzle was unraveling. She felt an incredible urge to say something, but she didn't know where to begin, how to interrupt what was going on in a powerful realm to which she was a visiting guest.

"What do y'all think?" Taylor murmured when the final, melodic note of the first cut on the gospel tape ended.

"Sensational!"

"A star waiting to be born!"

"With a voice like that, and additional mixes, and I'll put the talent of our mix-men against any residing in Boston, with the correct hype and the right image-making, we could shoot her across the pop, country, and gospel charts like has been done with Lee Ann Rimes and several others."

"A video deal, too, for her looks do justice to the voice. I could see it as a poignant stroll down country lanes, pastoral scenes, brush-arbor photography that would take people back to their roots, the rhythms, and the real meaning of what the verses of well-loved hymns mean to them."

"Autobiographies of singers have been a good tie-in lately, too. Actually, for quite some time," said a nattily dressed gentleman who'd been busy scribbling notes with a pen that Carli had become aware, since her move to Boston, had cost more than many families spent for a month's rent and groceries.

"Not to mention tee shirts," another added.

"Even a clothing line."

"Let's not get too far ahead of ourselves here," Tay cautioned. "I just wanted to give y'all a sample of what we have. Carli's verbally agreed over the telephone to go with Rising Star. Once the contracts that are being prepared even as we speak are signed and it's official, we'll be ready to talk deals, boys. So start getting your packages and offers together so we can get down to talking brass tacks about recording dates and record releases."

Nodding, offering words of agreement and promises to bid their best, the men departed, shaking hands with Carli on the way out, and speaking friendly words to Tay who clearly held authority in the stellar word of creating the stars who shone around the world.

"Well, Carli," Tay said when they were alone with Paige, "what do you think?"

"I think that you're very good at what you do."

"Thank you."

"But Tay, this is some kind of mistake—"

"You can't get cold feet now, Carli. I know that it's a bit overwhelming. You were confident enough this morning. As it so happened, I already had the meeting scheduled, so I figured let them see the newest singer arriving in Nashville with their very own eyes as they listened to the demo tape."

"You don't understand, Tay," Carli persisted. "I had no

idea what you were even talking about. You see, Tay, I left Boston before I received any kind of letter from you. . ."

"You what?" he inquired, his voice faint, as if the breath had been knocked out of him.

Carli repeated herself.

"Oh. . .no. . ." he said. "I had done some preliminary groundwork, and made you an offer by mail, batting the ball into your park. When you called me, I assumed that—well, you can see what I assumed."

"Yes, I can."

"What're we going to do?" Taylor asked.

Paige stood by as if she were transfixed by the most fantastic dramatic scene she'd ever witnessed as she realized what would rise or fall on Carli's response.

"I. . .I wouldn't know what to do."

Paige seemed to sense her opportunity. "That's why you'd have a manager," she said. "Someone to professionally hold your hand and guide you every step of the way."

"But—"

"You could do it, Carli," Taylor assured. "Simply sing your heart out for the Lord."

"I could do that," she observed.

"Sing your heart out for the Lord," Tay said, his voice holding a tinge of bitterness. "And do it for as long as worldly mankind involved in the music industry will allow you to do it. I won't lie to you, my friend, this is a dog-eat-puppy-business. Stars used to be considered born talents. Now stars are made. Created with cash in the boardrooms of publishers and producers with high-tech people hired to make even a median-sound singer star-quality, and a born singer into a superstar."

"Tay, you're scaring me. I don't know what to do."

"I'd suggest that you sing for the Lord, bank the money that comes in, face the reality that it won't last forever. . . maybe not even for very long. . .and then turn back to what it is that you really want to do in life. . .how you want to minister to people."

"I don't know what to say," Carli repeated.

"And, I won't ask you to sign a contract, and certainly won't pressure you to affix your name on the dotted line. Not until you've had some time to think about it, talk about it with those whose opinions matter, and at least overnight to take it to prayer with the Lord."

"That's reasonable."

"Don't worry about me, Carli, if you have to turn us down, although I'd very much like to help introduce you to the listening world. If you can't. . .no hard feelings. . .and just leave it up to me to make explanations to the gentlemen gathered at the meeting this evening."

"All right," Carli said.

"But don't forget, honey," Paige chimed in. "When opportunity knocks, it's generally a good idea to open the door. It frequently never comes calling again."

"Did you make the reservations as I asked?" Taylor faced Paige.

"Sure did, Boss," she said. "Just as you specified."

"Terrific."

"I've got some business to attend to before quitting time," he said, consulting a wristwatch that was serviceable but not one that flaunted wealth, although Carli knew Tay could've afforded a status symbol timepiece if he'd wanted to. "Would you take Carli to the apartment and show her around?"

"My pleasure," Paige said, and Carli knew that it wasn't just a pat phrase, Paige really meant it. There was something about Paige that had reached out and enveloped her in reassuring warmth and companionship. Given time she believed they could become close and trusted friends.

eighteen

Carli was startled to realize that she wouldn't have to juggle time to arrange for a visit with her aunts on the following day, because when Taylor escorted her into the elegant restaurant, there sat a beaming Eula Mae, and an equally radiant Fanchon, dressed in their Sunday best, and thoroughly enjoying the moment.

Carli gave them hugs and kisses, then accepted the chair that Taylor held for her.

"We had our first limousine ride!" Eula Mae excitedly told Carli. "We'll have another when we're returned to Golden Oaks."

"He's treating us with style, that boy," Fanchon said. She waggled a finger at him. "But I must admit, for some new high and mighty ways, he's still as common and comfortable as an old shoe. He's stuck with the ways of his raising."

"Thanks to the example of my parents," Taylor gave credit. "And people like Carli's folks and yourselves who were part of the Christian community in which I was raised."

"A nice community, too, wasn't it?"

"That's why I still get the old hometown paper," Tay said.

"Well, we were sure thrilled to see that write-up about you," Eula Mae said.

"And glad that we sent you a congratulations card, like folks back home tended to do."

"I'm glad, too."

"Well, a man as busy and as important as you didn't have to take the time to come visit a couple of old maids from his hometown, you know. But you did."

"And glad for it. I enjoyed seeing you—and never dreamed that I'd have Carli back in my life after all these years. I'll bet she doesn't even remember when she was in high school choir and I used to tell her she was good enough to go professional."

"Actually, I don't," Carli admitted.

Tay gave her a look. "That scares me! What else will you have forgotten that I told you in all seriousness, at times baring my heart and thoughts to you—?"

"Carli had a lot on her mind," Eula Mae defended, "what with the situation with her folks already begun. . ."

"Yes," Carli said. "Sometimes those days are a bit hazy."

She realized that she'd had some experience in shutting down emotionally and blocking out the painful elements of reality that she couldn't fully deal with. But, like a filter, the sadness was muted, but so were the glorious and happy moments.

"If you have any lapses, my dear, I can remind you. Just take my word for it."

"Trust? One should be able to trust an agent. And must be able to trust an agent," Paige chimed in as she was shown to their table.

The evening was pleasant, and Carli relaxed. They lingered for a long, long time, chatting, after other restaurant guests had departed.

The limousine was waiting to return her aunts to Golden Oaks, which was a wonderful and comfortable assisted living residence in a good neighborhood, a place where her aunts liked living and which Carli knew she'd enjoy visiting.

Her apartment, to which Tay was driving her, was nice, but there was an element of lush impersonality to it, which she realized she might not be around long enough to change, even if she felt the need in the sublet apartment that was as lovely and ready for her to take up residence as Taylor had promised.

Tay parked in the lot of the apartment complex. Carli felt unnerved. Would he hint to be invited up? He cleared his throat preparing to speak. Carli flinched with dread and a thousand excuses seemed to swirl through her mind.

"I'm sorry about your marriage, Carli," Tay began. "Your aunts told me that things weren't going well."

"Thank you for your concern."

"I do care, you know. I care about you. And because I care

about you, I also care about someone you love, even if I've never met him. Is there anything I can do? Any way I can help?"

"I don't know."

"I'm there for you, Carli. A shoulder to cry on if you need it, someone to listen to you. Someone to offer you a man's point of view. We're different, so pop psychologists and everyone else tells us, in every book and magazine, and on every talk show. As if the Lord didn't point that out in Genesis!"

Carli laughed.

"As you've noticed, Carli, I'm quite good at what I do. I've negotiated a lot of deals. If the time comes when you'd like to have me do something—put out feelers—to reach a reconciliation in your marriage, well, just say the word. And I wouldn't even bill you for a percentage of the gains," he teased.

"I appreciate the offer," Carli said.

"I have a feeling that I won't have to approach your husband," Tay assured. "Only a fool would let you get away. If he comes to Nashville and is here on bended knee to woo you back, the deal can still work out for a music ministry, Carli. You'd only have to come here periodically. And if you're required to go out on the road a lot, well—"

"We'll face that bridge when we come to it," Carli said.

"Just so we understand each other. I don't believe in divorce," Tay said. "But living the life of a separated wife isn't what I'd wish for you, either."

"Thanks for everything, Tay," Carli whispered. "I really must go in. I have some calls to make even though it's late."

"Good night, Carli," Tay said and pressed a kiss to her cheek as he gave her shoulder a friendly pat. "And God bless."

"Good night, old friend," Carli said, softly sighing.

"Old?" the Taylor Hayes she'd known so long squawked with feigned umbrage. "I'll inform you, Miss Star in the Making, I am exactly four months and seventeen days older than you are! I'm hardly an old man. Any more cheesy remarks like that one—and if you last in this biz 'til you're old and gray I'll order the company publicists to tell everyone your true age!"

"Some things never change," Carli laughed. "You're still a nut. Please stay that way."

"If you'll stay as sweet as you are," the professional negotiator automatically came back with an offer.

"It's a done deal!" Carli agreed.

She found she was still laughing to herself as she inserted her key into the lock and fumbled to get it open.

"Home, sweet home," she sighed, the way she and Gus had both done when returning from work shifts to their small apartment in Virginia.

She thought of the people back in Boston that had been a technical home but had failed to be a haven from the world. She called Jasper Winthrop's number, even though it was late, and was grateful he was still up.

"Hi, Uncle Jasper. I'm sorry for calling so late, but I wanted to contact you so that you wouldn't worry."

"Worry, Carli? Are you all right? What's wrong?"

"To make a long story short, Uncle Jasper, I'm going to turn up missing, probably tomorrow afternoon at the latest, if it's not discovered sooner."

It was clear she was confusing him as badly as she'd felt that Tay had errantly and innocently caused her puzzlement.

"I'm not in Boston. I'm in Nashville," she quickly started to give details. "I'm going to be signing a recording contract tomorrow."

"A recording contract! Wonderful! But how did that happen!"

Carli sketched in the series of events, which had begun when he'd suggested she sing a collection of songs to be recorded for Austin Dennis's enjoyment.

"Please don't tell Gus where I'm at," Carli said. "I realize that's asking a lot of you. But it's important to me. If Gus comes after me I want it to be because he really wants me back, not because someone's told him where I am and he feels he must do the socially acceptable thing, keep appearances up, and. . ."

"I understand perfectly," he agreed. "But do stay in touch."

"I will."

"There are many ways Gus can find you, Carli, other than having a caring old man give him a tip regarding the matter."

"I know."

"Gus has so many business decisions to make. There's a personal choice he must make as well."

"I know," Carli said, helpless to keep the bleakness she felt at the thought of Lauren from her tone.

"I'll be praying he makes the right one."

No sooner had Carli hung up from talking with Jasper than she phoned Sharon Hathaway, who wasn't surprised to hear from Carli, but was astounded to learn she was calling long distance from Nashville.

There was so much to share that Carli wasn't surprised when they stayed on the line for almost two hours, sharing everything in detail, even the sordid tape which Carli had been unable to finish watching, and had accidentally left in the VCR when she fled, so that the truth of what had driven her away would no doubt eventually come to light.

"Stay in touch," Sharon urged, as had Jasper.

"I will. And I'm giving you my telephone number so you can reach out and touch me, too."

"Terrific."

"I'm sure that in filling out paperwork with the Agency they'll have the standard forms that must be completed. If it's all right with you, in addition to listing my aunts, I'll put you down as someone to notify in case of an emergency. I could put down Jasper, but he's not a young man. If there's something that's an emergency dire enough so that Gus must be told I can trust you to do it. And I won't fear upsetting an elderly man who needs peace and serenity, not possible disasters and disruptions."

"You've got it, kid," Sharon promised. "Don't forget me when you're famous."

"I couldn't do it if I tried," Carli laughed. "We're sisters, you know. Joined in Christ, and bound by love."

"If we want to get technical about it, Carli," Sharon said, "we're not just mere sisters. We're sisters who are Siamese twins because the way we think alike we're joined at the head and joined at the heart."

"It's going to kill me that we won't be able to do lunch the way we've enjoyed."

"Let me know when you hit the concert circuit," Sharon said. "I'll keep track of the dates, and I promise you, when you're appearing within decent distance of Boston—I'll be there!"

"Let's not get ahead of ourselves," Carli cautioned, for it was as if she were constantly pinching herself to make certain that it wasn't just a dream from which she'd awaken.

"All I can say, Carli, is that you'd better brace yourself for what's to come, because when a servant of God listens, and then says yes to the call, well, grab your hat, Carli, and hang on for the ride, because He can open doors and create opportunities that no man could conceive in the guy's wildest imaginings of success."

✍

Weeks later, it was as if Sharon Hathaway's words that late night had been prophetic. Carli had signed the contract. Tay had negotiated the best deal in town.

The recording dates were set, the gospel material for the album selected, musicians auditioned to put together just the right band to produce the sound that they wanted to create to accompany Carli Waggoner's musical delivery, and much, much more.

There were photo shoots, interviews, meeting important people in the industry.

Then there was the time stolen away to visit her aunts and regularly attend church services where people didn't know what plans were in the making for her, and simply loved and accepted her for who she was. She prayed that it wouldn't change if fame came her way, and she believed it would not, for there were a lot of wonderful and dedicated Christians who populated the buildings that created Music Row and those involved in related industries.

There were calls to return, letters to respond to, people she was scheduled to meet. But each day seemed to be a disappointment, for there was no communication from Gus, whom she knew could have tracked her down within forty-eight hours or less if he'd had the mind to do it. And that hurt, knowing that maybe he was happier with her gone from his life when it seemed every day she grieved for the Gus she'd married and the relationship that they'd once had.

Carli buried herself in her work, realizing on a personal level how work had been like a pain numbing, self-administered option to the pain of his return to Boston only to face that he was about to lose the comforting presence of his father.

With Tay negotiating the deals and protecting her interest, and with Paige as her personal manager, Carli's career soared until it was the talk of the industry. The first time she interviewed for a trade newspaper had been exciting. Soon, however, the new wore off and she considered it a drag, but something she had to do, for the fans must be served.

There were a few times when she felt exhausted, and wished she could push a button and go back to before she'd signed the multipaged contract of legalese, but that was not to be.

She simply couldn't walk away from it. Too many people relied on her. It was as if, in being called a "musical property," which seemed to reduce her to such inhuman sounding terms, she was like a living, breathing corporation. If she simply decided she'd like to quit, while it was a price she could pay, she couldn't do that to the people who relied on her and had families to support, mortgages to pay, children to raise.

Once again, through personal experience, she came to understand the crushing weight of responsibility Gus felt. If he walked away, Dennis Mining and Manufacturing took a plunge because of edgy stockholders, it could harm countless people, and result in major calamities in their lives.

She understood so many things, now. But it was too late. Gus hadn't come after her; clearly he had reached a decision. He wanted Lauren and her modern, liberal, New Age lifestyle.

For three months Carli worked harder than she'd ever worked in her life. Everyone was thrilled after her album's release and were making plans for another recording session.

First they wanted her to go out on the road, and were considering setting up schedules, which would be well into the next seasoning schedule. But then as misfortune befell another Christian female artist, Carli's chance appeared.

"She's going to recover, thank the Lord," Tay said as he explained the situation, and how the singer had contracted hepatitis while overseas, and her condition was such that it'd be a long time before she had the strength to return to the stage. "Rather than cancel the scheduled shows, we'd like to switch her tour over to make it the Carli Waggoner tour. What do you say?"

"What should I say, Tay?"

"The smart career move is to go for it. Say yes."

"Then yes it is," is what Carli had always agreed. But this time, she couldn't, and, although she could tell that Tay was a bit disappointed, she asked for a couple of days to think it over. At that moment she could understand perfectly how Gus could fall asleep fully clothed, sitting up in a chair, with the lights on and papers in his grip.

She called Sharon with the news of the offer, and promised that if she agreed to go on the road, she'd send her a concert itinerary as soon as she was apprised of the scheduled dates.

"Congratulations, Carli!" Sharon cried. "You'll have your name up in lights just like someone else that you know."

"Who?" Carli inquired.

"Lauren Beekman. . ."

At the mention of her name Carli felt as if she had suffered a blow to the chest that made her heart falter.

"What's she up to now?"

"Mmmmm. Appearing on Broadway, it seems, according to a write-up in *The Globe*."

"No kidding."

"Nope, kiddo. Serious as a heart attack, I am. She's making it big on Broadway."

"I knew that she enjoyed acting. She and Gus had that in common during their teenage years and community theater projects."

"Apparently she's good," Sharon said.

"I'm sure that she is," Carli said, her tone helplessly stiff and cold at the ideas that returned to nettle her mind.

"From the article in the newspaper, Gus can't be too bad a hand on stage behind the footlights himself."

"What are you talking about?" Carli inquired.

"I may as well break it to you, Carli. In the newspaper article, Lauren credits Gus Dennis, and the staff at Dennis Mining and Manufacturing, with her getting a big break and the opportunity to audition for the part she landed."

"How interesting. I'm sure Gus loved assisting her."

"I think it was strictly business for him. A favor. You see, as it turns out, there seems to be this video, which was referred to several times in the article. This professionally produced video, in which she portrays the romantic lead, and her old acting buddy Gus Dennis plays the part of the leading man, was enough to convince the producers on Broadway to give her a chance."

Carli began to tremble.

"Oh, Sharon. . .no. . .no. . ."

"Yes, I'm afraid it's true, Carli. The videotape produced in the den of the Dennis mansion, created with the help of portable equipment, and a lone cameraman, then produced by the production team at the corporate headquarters was superb enough to convince the producers to give Lauren a chance—"

"And realistic enough to make me believe that Gus was cheating on me. . ."

"It was a natural conclusion, honey," Sharon sympathized. "Even if it was wrong. Gus didn't have time to mention that he'd assisted his lifelong friend with a video sample of her acting ability. He knew about the tape, obviously. But someone else knew how damaging it could be if it came to your attention in the wrong way."

"Who?"

"I'd cast my vote that it wasn't Lauren, for the article refers to some leading man with whom she's been involved, with their taking in the nightspots and getting a bit of coverage in the society and gossip columns."

"Mitzi. It had to have been Mitzi."

"That'd be who'd win my vote."

Carli began to cry.

"Doesn't she have any care, any concern for who all she hurts?"

Feeling helpless to stop, she railed on and on about Gus's mother, feeling the feelings, expressing the anger, recognizing the depth of emotion in the things she'd tried to ignore but realized she'd simply set aside, as if to deal with later, and now found that it was like an ugly reservoir of hurts stored up that had grown daily.

"Doesn't she care who she destroys if she gets her way? Has that woman no conscience whatsoever?"

There was a moment of silence as Carli's words seemed to echo over the fiber-optic wires like an anguished howl.

"A week ago I'd have fully agreed with you, and felt that she didn't care, and that she had no conscience. . ." Her words trailed off.

"And—" Carli found herself prompting.

"And in the meantime, things have changed. Mrs. Dennis has changed."

Carli had a hard time believing that, but said nothing.

"Due to patient confidentiality, Carli, there are so many things I can't say. But a few that I can. Please, don't ask me for details you know that I'm not free to provide."

"What are you trying to tell me?"

"Mrs. Dennis is my patient, Carli, in the private wing at the hospital."

"Oh my—"

"Don't ask!" Sharon pleaded. "Simply let me tell you what I safely can."

"Is she—" Then Carli swallowed further words, not wanting to make the choices any more difficult that they already were for her trusted friend.

"She's my patient, Carli, and now she's my sister in Christ."

"How did that happen?" Carli gasped.

She could hear Sharon's smile over the miles before she spoke. "In the usual way, of course, she gave her heart and life to Jesus Christ and accepted that He died on the Cross to pay the penalty of her sins."

"I know how it happened. But I want to know how. Don't torment me!"

"When she was hospitalized, well, Jasper witnessed to her. I witnessed to her. And so did Gus."

"Praise God!"

"But it was you, Carli, who did the most to bring her to the Lord. The testimony of your songs sang her all the way to salvation as they served to sing Austin Dennis into the arms of the Lord. I guess that I can safely tell you that her condition is stable, and she's going to recover. But it was nip-and-tuck there for a while. We didn't know if Mrs. Dennis was going to make it. We had to commit her life to the Lord, just as she had done. He brought her through the crisis and I think one that really gave her the will to die when she could've gone Home to her Savior."

"Really?" Carli murmured.

"More than anything, Carli, she hopes to one day apologize to you for all the things she said and did."

Tears were burning in Carli's eyes.

"I owe several people heartfelt apologies myself," Carli softly wept.

"We all do," Sharon soothed. "We're only human. The views as seen from a worldly perspective can make us blind to what God would have us see."

"That's surely been true," Carli said. "But Gus—I left. . . he never tried to contact me. Why?"

"Because he was feeling quite rejected himself, Carli. As a child sometimes he was an inconvenience to his frivolous mother. He was ignored by a father who was buried in work. Gus learned long ago that if someone didn't have the time for him, didn't want to be around him, then he'd make himself scarce and stay out of the way. He loves you, Carli. But feeling that you no longer love or want him as your husband, his pride is such that he can't risk seeking out only to be turned away."

"Sharon, why didn't you tell me these things!" Carli demanded.

"I did!" she protested. "During some of our coffee chats I explained human psychology in some detail."

"I'm sorry," Carli apologized. "I guess you did. I guess that I was unwilling to listen to what I was too steeped in hurt to even hear."

"You've grown a lot. Gus has too. With the news you told me about the tour, well, Carli, I felt that I had to share these things with you, so that whatever you choose to do you can make an educated decision."

"One educated decision I've reached, Sharon, is that I have been a fool."

"That's in the past," Sharon reminded.

"I wonder if I even have a future."

"You sure do, Caroline Waggoner Dennis. And it's up to you which one you choose. . ."

With that, Sharon yawned, bid a quick good night, and then almost hung up on Carli, no doubt aware as Sharon tucked herself into bed in Boston that her chum in Nashville would face a sleepless night as she wrestled with possibilities, knew the answers couldn't be wrought from her own human frailties, but would have to be choices aligned with the Lord's perfect will.

At that moment, Carli drifted off to sleep: soothed, serene, secure and so very, very happy. She would give Tay her answer tomorrow. And by the following evening, Lord willing, post the most important question she could inquire of her husband: Did he still want her as his wife?

nineteen

Due to family obligations to Gus, that had arisen in Carli with her call to Sharon, and comforted and encouraged by all that Sharon Hathaway had shared, Carli had known what she had to do. It had given her the answer to the opportunity that Tay had presented for her consideration while needing a quick decision.

She'd placed a call to Tay at his home, contacting him more as a friend than as a Rising Star Entertainment Agency client. He'd asked if she was free to go out for dinner, suggested he pick her up, and they could dine together and talk about it all.

Carli unburdened her heart just as soon as the waitress had taken their order. She shared bits about her past, what she had been going through, and she explained her hopes, dreams, desires, and voiced the fears and uncertainties that sometimes almost paralyzed her into inaction.

She was fearful that heavy involvement in the professional recording industry could cause her to change from who she was, and who she wanted to be, and who she felt the Lord wanted her to become. Due to pressures and commitments to others, to her fans, to the record company executives, she feared that her commitment to the Lord might be overshadowed by commitment to bottom-line figures.

"I've sensed what's happened to some of the people I've already met," she murmured. "They have no time for their families unless they take them out on the road. They haven't stable enough routines to attend a church regularly and be active in church family life. And—"

On and on Carli talked, hastily sketching in what she'd analyzed about the Christian music industry, that she feared sometimes wasn't as Christian as it should be in practice, with behaviors that were as cutthroat and cruel as behaviors by unchurched and agnostic business persons in other industries.

"I wish I could tell you that you were wrong, Carli," Taylor said, nodding. "But you're not. It's frequently not a pretty business, and sometimes rather than being inspiring, it's dirty, demoralizing, and frustrating. The industry powers know that they can make a star—and they also know that they can break a star. They can kill off the career of someone who chooses not to play by their rules. You're right."

"I don't want that," Carli said.

"I don't want that for you."

"I don't want singing to be a job. I want it to be something to always enjoy, to marvel at what I feel is a gift made to be shared with others."

Taylor smiled. "Your instincts are correct, Carli. For many people, although they are unaware of it, they are like goldfish being tossed into a shark tank. Some will do anything to survive. Others won't. And if they make it from the shark tank alive, they find themselves forever changed. Not for the better, either."

"I guess what I'm trying to say is that I have decided that as good as the opportunity sounds in some ways, I can't do it."

"After all that you've just shared, I wouldn't want you to. And, in some ways that's a relief to me."

"Relief?" Carli murmured.

Taylor lowered his voice, then looked around. "I know that you'll realize what I'm about to say is off the record, Carli, so I won't go through the usual song-and-dance swearing you to secrecy and reminding you of confidentiality ethics."

She nodded. "Go ahead."

"I've been thinking for some time of leaving the Agency."

"Taylor!" she gasped, shocked. He was good at what he did, and she had believed he thrived on the high-stress situations.

"It's true," he said.

Then he unburdened himself of all that had built up within him, which he'd tried to ignore and pretend wasn't there.

"I want to climb out of the shark-tank situations and live a normal life," he said. "Find a good woman. Settle down in some nice neighborhood, find something that provides a living in addition to what I've saved up over the years. Have a family. You know, the American Dream. . .but with a Christian spin, so to speak."

"Sounds good, Tay, because that's what I want. And I'm hoping it's what my husband still desires."

"Now, to find the woman. And a place to relocate. I can't stay here. I could get sucked back into it too easily."

Suddenly something within Carli clicked.

"Have I got a woman for you!" she cried, thinking of Sharon Hathaway.

She interrupted Taylor's private reflections to rush on with a thumbnail sketch of Sharon's attractions.

"She sounds like a dream come to life."

"She is. Interested in meeting her sometime?"

"I think so."

As Taylor spoke on, Carli realized that with his various capabilities, he would be able to find employment, especially in a metropolitan area, that would put to use his considerable talents and that he wouldn't be simply leaving a well-paying occupation to barely scrape by elsewhere.

"I know that I'm meant to use my singing talent," Carli said. "But to be quite honest. . .I'm not at all comfortable with the 'star' treatment. I think that the focus should be on the Lord as my Savior not on me as 'the star'."

"I like that view," Taylor said. "It's a pity that more people don't share it. But a lot of Christian singers do, you know, and they have their special areas in Christian music, on a more grassroots level, where the gifts that God has given them are used for Christian inspiration and edification. There's a place for you, Carli, but which would allow you to first and foremost be the wife, mother, helpmate, and friend that you feel the Lord called you to be."

"What do you mean?"

Then Tay began to explain about the many gospel groups and the singers that he was aware of, who were located all over the geography of the United States. They were well-known as gospel singers in their own regions, singing at churches, paying expenses through love offerings from small congregations to help them with their expenses, and having available independent label cassette disks and tapes so that listeners could enjoy their songs anytime they wished.

"That sounds wonderful," Carli said.

"They'll never make the numbers on industry charts, but they're doing something lasting and wonderful. They're serving the Lord as they desire, and they're aware that no big city executive can decide that one day they're in and a hot property, and the next week they're all but thrown out into the street, robbed of star treatment, stripped of recognition, wondering what to do."

"That would make a person feel horrible to have that happen."

"And it does," Taylor quietly stressed. "Have you noticed over recent years, Carli, how hot properties are only good to remain in the spotlight's focus before pretty soon they are replaced and you don't hear much about them unless they're appearing locally on the county-fair circuit."

Carli's thoughts flooded back, and to her shock, she realized he was right. She was familiar with country and western artists, who had had crossover gospel albums when she was a child, some of her father's favorite singers. She began to name them.

"Dead in the water," Taylor sadly said, over and over and over again, and Carli knew that he spoke the truth.

Her heart felt pity for these talented singers, who'd given their all, even had faith in record companies, only to find themselves betrayed in the end, dismissed, with no gratitude for how they'd helped various labels amass fortunes in past decades, and make way for the newcomers selected to be "in" for awhile, then on their way "out" to make room for the next manmade stars.

"With your talent you could serve the Lord. You might not be singing in concert halls to sell-out crowds. But you'd find a warm and hearty welcome in churches where you'd share your gift."

"I think I'd like that."

"Your husband could go with you for companionship."

Carli suddenly laughed. "I'd put him to work!" she grinned.

"Work?" Tay questioned, not quite sure what she meant.

"He sings. We sing. He's very, very good."

"This I've got to hear!" Tay said.

"You should. But I don't know when you'll get the chance."

"When are you returning to Boston, Carli?" Tay had asked.

"In the morning."

"If you don't mind, I'll book passage on that flight, too," he said. "I haven't had a vacation in quite a while. It seems that there are people in Boston I'd really like to meet. It's a town I need to look over. With cell phones, fax machines, and modern technology, I can conduct business long distance for a few days."

"I'd love to have you come along," Carli said, "and there's plenty of space at the Dennis mansion."

"Be sure to tell your aunts where you'll be," Taylor reminded.

Carli paused. "I wonder if they'd like to tag along."

"They'd love it," Tay predicted. "You convince them to pack their bags, and I'll arrange for three seats on the airplane. My treat!"

"Everyone's treat!" Carli corrected. "What fun this will be."

❧

Carli's heart was thumping so hard that when the jet's wheels bumped against the tarmac at Logan International Airport she scarcely even noticed.

Taylor gave Carli a reassuring smile and squeezed her hand in a gesture of encouragement. Aunts Eula Mae and Fanchon were too excited to really notice Carli's trepidation.

"Where to?" Taylor inquired when they'd collected their baggage and were standing curbside as taxicabs lined up to collect fares and transport them to diverse destinations. "The mansion? Or the hospital?" He seemed to prod a decision from Carli.

She swallowed hard. "The hospital. . ."

The cab driver stowed their luggage then solicitously helped them into his vehicle.

Eula Mae and Fanchon were so excited at seeing a new city, and one so rich in the nation's history, that Carli found their enthusiasm a pleasant diversion from her private fears and misgivings.

"Everything's going to work out fine," Tay assured in a tone so low that it was only for Carli's hearing.

Wordlessly she looked at him.

Would it?

She owed so many apologies to Gus. The very things that had so irritated, frustrated, discouraged, and frightened her about his behavior turned out to be the same actions to which she had resorted. When the pressures became great and they failed to defuse the emotionally volatile situations through honestly talking and discussing their feelings, her own choices and reactions had been as unhealthy as Gus's behaviors.

Would he forgive her? Would he meet her halfway? Would he still feel the commitment to their holy vows of marriage as she? Would he be as prepared as she was now to truly honor their vows? Taking each other. . .in sickness and in health. . .for richer or for poorer. . .for better or worse. . . until death parted?

She knew her own heart and mind. Fervently she prayed that Gus had had time to think, feel, and would be as resolved as she to recapture what it seemed they had lost but could have as theirs forever and ever, come what may, whether enjoying blessings or sustaining one another through trials and testing.

It felt almost like a homecoming when the driver deposited them in front of the main entrance to the hospital. Taylor, bless his heart, took control of the situation and made arrangements with the desk clerk in the lobby to store their luggage behind the counter until they were ready to collect it and depart for the Dennis mansion.

They crossed to the elevators. Carli's stomach was already fluttering with butterflies that she didn't even notice the usual sinking sensation as the enclosure smoothly and rapidly shot upwards.

The doors yawned open. Carli saw Sharon Hathaway bent over a computer keyboard. There was a look of astonished delight when she saw Carli and she leapt from her chair, enveloping her friend in a crushing hug.

Breathlessly Carli made introductions and while Sharon was solicitous of Carli's aunts, it was clear to Carli that from the moment she'd introduced Taylor and Sharon, they had eyes for only one another.

Sharon led the party down the corridor in the direction of Mitzi's room where Gus was visiting his mother.

"This is as far as we go, folks," Sharon announced. "Carli's going solo from this point."

Even as a frightened part of Carli protested, she knew her friend was right. Noiselessly she progressed the remaining distance and paused at the door that was half-closed. For a moment as she hesitated she felt stunned.

Familiar songs. . .

Familiar voice. . .

Familiar memories. . .

Carli Waggoner Dennis's first gospel album, produced by technicians at Dennis Mining and Manufacturing was playing in Mitzi Dennis's sickroom as it had in Austin's hospital quarters.

Carli could see Gus, whose back was to the door, and his mother, her features wan and pale from the draining tropical virus that afflicted her, her eyes closed, her face serene, as she visited with her son while her daughter-in-law's uplifting inspirational music softly filled the room.

Singing had become so much a part of Carli's life that she found herself singing along with her own album, doing what Skeeter Davis had made such a famous technique, when she sang harmony to her own voice.

Mitzi noticed the difference. Her eyes flipped open. Then they widened at the sight of Carli, and she blinked, as if fearing that Carli was a vision that would disappear. Then Mitzi's eyes filled with tears of regret and sorrow. Biting her lip, her eyes pleading, she opened her arms to Carli while a shadow of fear lingered, that she'd done too many horrible, hurtful, even unforgivable things in the past to even warrant a future relationship with her son's beloved.

Carli slipped into the older woman's embrace. Genuine feelings passed between them.

"Can you ever forgive me?" Mitzi whispered as the heat of her tears dampened Carli's cheeks. "I've sinned against the Lord. . .and against you. Please, oh please, find it within yourself to forgive me. . ."

Carli kissed Mitzi's wan cheek and cupped her chin in her palm.

"I already have," she said, her heart surging with joy that it was the truth, and she was freed of ugly old feelings as she was rejoicing in the Christ-born change and newness in the woman who was not only her mother-in-law but a sister in Christ.

"Carli, is it really you?" Gus whispered, as if he feared that he was dreaming and might awaken to find Carli gone.

She nodded. "I've come home to apologize for all of the—"

"I've prayed for your return so I could ask your forgiveness," Gus interrupted.

"You've had it without having to ask," she said, wiping her eyes as she slipped into his warm and waiting embrace, and lifted her lips to meet his.

"It's I who need to apologize and need forgiveness," Gus whispered against her lips.

"We both do," Carli said.

"We all do," Mitzi corrected. She reached for Carli's hand, then for her sons. Drawn to her, Carli realized that it was the first time they'd felt like. . .a family!

"Knock-knock!" Sharon Hathaway called out in a bright whisper. "More visitors!"

Carli made introductions. To Carli's relief, but not to her surprise, considering the depth of the changes in Mitzi, she and Eula Mae and Fanchon hit it off like lifelong chums.

"As an only child I always wanted big sisters," Mitzi said. "No doubt you two can teach me a lot. And you'll absolutely love Jasper Winthrop. He's like a caring brother for all of us!"

"We'll all enjoy getting to know one another," they agreed.

"In what remains of our time on earth," Mitzi promised, "and for all time in Glory."

A little while later, after ensuring that Mitzi was settled in for the night's rest, the group left the hospital for the Dennis home. Once they arrived and placed their belongings in the various quarters and guest suites, they gathered in the ornately decorated parlor.

Not surprisingly they stayed up most of the night talking. Taylor and Gus hit it off as businesspersons. Tay was someone Gus felt he could confide in, to plan strategy for the Dennis firm. And Sharon, who arrived after her shift ended, wide-eyed at the luxury of the Dennis mansion, was clearly as smitten by Taylor as he was by her.

Carli just knew their brand-new friendship was going to blossom and grow.

And, it was an answer to prayer when Gus and she lay awake talking until almost dawn, hands clasped closely as they shared their hopes, their dreams, their fears, and their feelings.

"There's a family tradition," Gus said. "And a faith tradition."

"I know," Carli said.

Gus began to explain the concepts that had so recently been impressed upon her heart by the Lord.

"I know," she said.

"How can you know?" he queried.

Carli finished up the philosophies about family tradition and a tradition of faith, and that regardless of the length or the lineage, the Lord's tradition must be honored before family tradition.

"It was like I was railroaded into the family business because of tradition. Choices were made for me before I was even born. I don't want that. And I certainly don't want it for my children. I want my family members to be free to be whoever or whatever the Lord would will them to be."

"That's what I want, too."

"I've talked about it with Mom," Gus said. "We've decided to sell our interest in Dennis Mining and Manufacturing, keep the mansion, at least for a while, but do something else with our money and lives."

"Oh. . .Gus!"

"And, after meeting your old friend from Kentucky," Gus said, "I recognize in Taylor Hayes exactly the kind of person I would want on my team."

"Did you think that Sharon and Tay were attracted to each other?" Carli asked Gus what had seemed apparent to her.

"I think he sees in Sharon exactly the kind of woman he'd want for a wife."

"The Lord has a plan. I know He does."

"Be patient, my sweet, and 'twill be revealed."

"My aunts love it here," Carli said. "I'm so glad. They're both so healthy it seems a shame that they pay such sums to live in an assisted living residence."

"Convince them to relocate to Boston and us here at the mansion, and they won't have to," Gus reasoned. "We have enough staff members to do all the 'assisting' they would need."

"Oh, but pray that they'd agree to that," Carli said. "I'd love having family close by. I felt so sad having to leave your mother at the hospital when all of us were coming here. I know how much she wanted to come along."

"I felt that too," Gus said. "She could come home, if she had private-duty nursing staff that was really good."

"Sharon Hathaway!" they exclaimed together.

"You know. . .she might consider it. Sharon says nursing isn't what it used to be, either, due to budget cuts, all the new health plans, and insurance regulated stay-times for so many things."

"It won't hurt to ask," Gus decided.

"I know what I'll be praying she says!"

epilogue

Boston
One Year Later

Gus lovingly supported Carli's elbow after helping her into the new, satiny robe and matching slippers. They left the pleasant, quiet hospital room she shared with another new mother who was napping.

Carli's slippers scuffed on the gleaming floor of the hospital corridor. Gus's steps clacked on the highly buffed surface as he solicitously measured his pace to hers.

"I've never loved you more than I do at this moment. And, I've loved you a lot and for a long, long time."

"I know," Carli said, and twined her fingers with his.

She knew that due to the past two days in the hospital, she didn't look as attractive as she might have liked, but she also was aware that Gus was blinded to any imperfections present, and that he considered her the most wondrous, most interesting, bravest, most exciting, desirable woman alive: his wife.

And now the mother of his children.

Carli was misty-eyed with overwhelming good emotions that made her heart seem to blossom even more full with the wondrous, blessedness of it all.

Ah, to experience, savor, and know to the full such miraculous and God-given feelings.

She, Gus, his mother, Jasper, Sharon, even Taylor Hayes and her aunts had all walked through dark, shadowy valleys of uncertainty, relying on the inner Light of the Lord to lead them correctly, when humanly they had felt lost and without direction in the worldly gloom that had pressed in all around, causing them to honor the past, inventory the present, and consider the future and God's perfect will for them.

So much had happened in the past twelve months, so many blessings, and it had resulted in the beginning of new family and business traditions based on faith, not habit.

Sharon Hathaway had become Mrs. Taylor Hayes, private-duty nurse at the Dennis mansion. She had overseen the return to full health of Mitzi Dennis. Then, when Jasper had suffered a stroke and fallen and injured himself, he came to live at the mansion with Sharon as his nurse.

It was a comfort to Carli's aunts to have a registered nurse nearby, and convenient for Tay and Sharon whose house was close to the mansion where they were frequent visitors. Close by, too, was the building Gus had purchased with a portion of the stock proceeds, as he and Taylor pooled their talents and knowledge and connections to do business on a more grassroots level and produce Christian artists' work, people who had a gift from God, who although they would never make the "big time," and didn't want to, wished to serve the Lord.

"Some traditions are good," Gus said as he and Carli gazed through the plate-glass nursery at their twins, a darling son and gorgeous little daughter."

"Others are made to be broken," she chimed in to finish the thought, "with choices to be made on a personal level with the Lord's guidance."

"That's all I could want for Nathan Austin Dennis. . ."

"And for his sister, Natalie Alexandra—"

"The most beautiful babies you ever saw," Mitzi Dennis said, having sneaked up behind them to put an arm around both her son and her daughter, a gift from the Lord to the Dennis family. "But then, of course, I'm prejudiced, you know," she said, beaming down at the twins, wiping tears of joy caused by the sight of them in their perfect innocence.

"Of course you are, Grandma," Gus said, and gave her a squeeze.

"Traditions," Mitzi Dennis sighed. "I overheard you talking about traditions. Having babies and raising them to worship and love the Lord Jesus, that's one that must go on!

We're all going to expect an encore, Carli."

Gus, the head of the family, spoke for the both of them.

"We'll do our best," he promised, as Carli laughed with agreement.

A Letter To Our Readers

Dear Reader:

In order that we might better contribute to your reading enjoyment, we would appreciate your taking a few minutes to respond to the following questions. When completed, please return to the following:

Rebecca Germany, Managing Editor
Heartsong Presents
PO Box 719
Uhrichsville, Ohio 44683

1. Did you enjoy reading *Once More With Feeling?*
   ❏ Very much. I would like to see more books by this author!
   ❏ Moderately
   I would have enjoyed it more if _____
   _____

2. Are you a member of **Heartsong Presents**? ❏ Yes ❏ No
   If no, where did you purchase this book? _____
   _____

3. What influenced your decision to purchase this book? (Check those that apply.)

   ❏ Cover   ❏ Back cover copy

   ❏ Title   ❏ Friends

   ❏ Publicity   ❏ Other_____

4. How would you rate, on a scale from 1 (poor) to 5 (superior), the cover design? _____

5. On a scale from 1 (poor) to 10 (superior), please rate the following elements.

    ___Heroine   ___Plot

    ___Hero   ___Inspirational theme

    ___Setting   ___Secondary characters

6. What settings would you like to see covered in **Heartsong Presents** books?_____

_____

_____

7. What are some inspirational themes you would like to see treated in future books?_____

_____

_____

8. Would you be interested in reading other **Heartsong Presents** titles?   ❑ Yes   ❑ No

9. Please check your age range:
   ❑ Under 18   ❑ 18-24   ❑ 25-34
   ❑ 35-45   ❑ 46-55   ❑ Over 55

10. How many hours per week do you read? _____

Name _____

Occupation_____

Address_____

City_____ State_____ Zip _____

Heartsong Presents Classics!

We have put together a collection of some of the most popular **Heartsong Presents** titles in two value-priced volumes. Favorite titles from our first year of publication, no longer published in single volumes, are now available in our new *Inspirational Romance Readers.*

Historical Collection #2 includes:

- ❤ *When Comes the Dawn* by Brenda Bancroft
- ❤ *The Sure Promise* by JoAnn A. Grote
- ❤ *Dream Spinner* by Sally Laity
- ❤ *Shores of Promise* by Kate Blackwell

Contemporary Collection #2 includes:

- ❤ *Design for Love* by Janet Gortsema
- ❤ *Fields of Sweet Content* by Norma Jean Lutz
- ❤ *From the Heart* by Sara Mitchell
- ❤ *Llama Lady* by VeraLee Wiggins

Each collection is $4.97 plus $1.00 for shipping and handling. Buy both collections for $8.99 plus $1.00 for shipping and handling.

Available through **Heartsong Presents**
toll-free 1-800-847-8270
or send orders to:
Heartsong Presents
P.O. Box 719
Uhrichsville, Ohio 44683
http://www.barbourbooks.com

Prices subject to change without notice.

Heart♥ng

**Any 12 Heartsong Presents titles for only $26.95 **

CONTEMPORARY ROMANCE IS CHEAPER BY THE DOZEN!

Buy any assortment of twelve Heartsong Presents titles and save 25% off of the already discounted price of $2.95 each!

**plus $1.00 shipping and handling per order and sales tax where applicable.

HEARTSONG PRESENTS *TITLES AVAILABLE NOW:*

___HP106 RAGDOLL, *Kelly R. Stevens*
___HP113 BETWEEN THE MEMORY AND THE MOMENT, *Susannah Hayden*
___HP118 FLICKERING FLAMES, *Connie Loraine*
___HP121 THE WINNING HEART, *Norma Jean Lutz*
___HP142 FLYING HIGH, *Phyllis A. Humphrey*
___HP149 LLAMA LAND, *VeraLee Wiggins*
___HP162 GOLDEN DREAMS, *Kathleen Yapp*
___HP166 A GIFT FROM ABOVE, *Dina Leonhardt Koehly*
___HP177 NEPALI NOON, *Susannah Hayden*
___HP178 EAGLES FOR ANNA, *Cathrine Runyon*
___HP181 RETREAT TO LOVE, *Nancy N. Rue*
___HP182 A WING AND A PRAYER, *Tracie J. Peterson*
___HP185 ABIDE WITH ME, *Una McManus*
___HP186 WINGS LIKE EAGLES, *Tracie J. Peterson*
___HP189 A KINDLED SPARK, *Colleen L. Reece*
___HP190 A MATTER OF FAITH, *Nina Coombs Pykare*
___HP193 COMPASSIONATE LOVE, *Ann Bell*

___HP194 WAIT FOR THE MORNING, *Kjersti Hoff Baez*
___HP197 EAGLE PILOT, *Jill Stengl*
___HP198 WATERCOLOR CASTLES, *Ranee McCollum*
___HP201 A WHOLE NEW WORLD, *Yvonne Lehman*
___HP202 SEARCH FOR TODAY, *Mary Hawkins*
___HP205 A QUESTION OF BALANCE, *Veda Boyd Jones*
___HP206 POLITICALLY CORRECT, *Kay Cornelius*
___HP209 SOFT BEATS MY HEART, *Aleesha Carter*
___HP210 THE FRUIT OF HER HANDS, *Jane Orcutt*
___HP213 PICTURE OF LOVE, *Tamela Hancock Murray*
___HP214 TOMORROW'S RAINBOW, *VeraLee Wiggins*
___HP217 ODYSSEY OF LOVE, *Melanie Panagiotopoulos*
___HP218 HAWAIIAN HEARTBEAT, *Yvonne Lehman*
___HP221 THIEF OF MY HEART, *Catherine Bach*
___HP222 FINALLY, LOVE, *Jill Stengl*
___HP225 A ROSE IS A ROSE, *Ruth Richert Jones*
___HP226 WINGS OF THE DAWN, *Tracie J. Peterson*

(If ordering from this page, please remember to include it with the order form.)

········ Presents ········

Great Inspirational Romance at a Great Price!

Heartsong Presents books are inspirational romances in contemporary and historical settings, designed to give you an enjoyable, spirit-lifting reading experience. You can choose wonderfully written titles from some of today's best authors like Veda Boyd Jones, Yvonne Lehman, Tracie Peterson, Nancy N. Rue, and many others.

When ordering quantities less than twelve, above titles are $2.95 each.
Not all titles may be available at time of order.

SEND TO: **Heartsong Presents** Reader's Service
P.O. Box 719, Uhrichsville, Ohio 44683

Please send me the items checked above. I am enclosing $_____
(please add $1.00 to cover postage per order. OH add 6.25% tax. NJ
add 6%.). Send check or money order, no cash or C.O.D.s, please.
To place a credit card order, call 1-800-847-8270.

NAME _____

ADDRESS _____

CITY/STATE _____ ZIP _____

Heart♥ng Presents
Love Stories Are Rated G!

That's for godly, gratifying, and of course, great! If you love a thrilling love story, but don't appreciate the sordidness of some popular paperback romances, **Heartsong Presents** is for you. In fact, **Heartsong Presents** is the *only inspirational romance book club*, the only one featuring love stories where Christian faith is the primary ingredient in a marriage relationship.

Sign up today to receive your first set of four, never before published Christian romances. Send no money now; you will receive a bill with the first shipment. You may cancel at any time without obligation, and if you aren't completely satisfied with any selection, you may return the books for an immediate refund!

Imagine. . .four new romances every four weeks—two historical, two contemporary—with men and women like you who long to meet the one God has chosen as the love of their lives. . .all for the low price of $9.97 postpaid.

To join, simply complete the coupon below and mail to the address provided. **Heartsong Presents** romances are rated G for another reason: They'll arrive *Godspeed!*

YES! Sign me up for Heart♥ng!

NEW MEMBERSHIPS WILL BE SHIPPED IMMEDIATELY!
Send no money now. We'll bill you only $9.97 post-paid with your first shipment of four books. Or for faster action, call toll free 1-800-847-8270.

NAME _____

ADDRESS _____

CITY _____ STATE _____ ZIP _____

MAIL TO: HEARTSONG PRESENTS, P.O. Box 719, Uhrichsville, Ohio 44683

YES10-96